“You mus[illegible] Suzie whispered[illegible]

Chris shook hi[illegible] ıer.”

She took a deep [illegible] ıe still felt as if she w[illegible] I must look like a mess.”

“Not possible,” he told her, taking out his handkerchief. Very carefully, his eyes on hers, he began to wipe away the tears from her cheeks. “See,” he murmured, “better already.”

Before he knew exactly how it happened, Chris found himself lowering his mouth to Suzie’s and kissing her. Kissing away her pain.

With what felt like the last ounce of his strength, Chris put his hands on her shoulders and drew her away from him.

“Suzie,” he cautioned. “You don’t want to do this.”

She felt bewildered and not a little stunned, as if she was being pulled in two different directions at once. “I don’t?”

“I mean, you don’t want to do something you’re going to regret.”

“Then don’t make me regret it,” she whispered, taking hold of the front of Chris’s shirt and pulling him to her. . .

* * *

Be sure to check out the next books in this exciting series: **Cavanaugh Justice**—Where Aurora’s finest are always in action

CAVANAUGH IN THE ROUGH

MARIE FERRARELLA

First Published in Great Britain 2017
By Mills & Boon, an imprint of HarperCollins*Publishers*
1 London Bridge Street, London, SE1 9GF

ISBN: 978-0-263-93032-0

18-0217

Our policy is to use papers that are natural, renewable and recyclable products and made from wood grown in sustainable forests.The logging and manufacturing processes conform to the legal environmental regulations of the country of origin.

Printed and bound in Spain
by CPI, Barcelona

USA TODAY bestselling and RITA® Award-winning author **Marie Ferrarella** has written more than two-hundred-and-fifty books for Mills & Boon, some under the name Marie Nicole. Her romances are beloved by fans worldwide. Visit her website, www.marieferrarella.com.

To

Susan Kyser Frank

For Always Having

Such Great Things to Say.

This One's For You

Prologue

A host of thoughts, mostly fragmented, were playing ping-pong in Detective Christian Cavanaugh O'Bannon's head as he drove to work. He was just a tad punchy, having gotten virtually no sleep. His goal was to go in early so that he could leave early and get his life back on track.

For now, that was the plan.

Last night's revelry was still clinging to him like the light scent of expensive perfume that sold by the fraction of an ounce. Perfume worn by the woman he'd been trying to corner at the party he'd attended. She'd been friendly and warm, and just when he thought he was finally getting somewhere, he'd turned around and she was gone.

He'd stuck around, thinking their paths would

cross again, but they hadn't. There'd been other single women there, just as attractive in their own way, but somehow he couldn't work up the enthusiasm about any of them the way he had about the one who "got away."

Consequently, he was still somewhat frustrated, as well as just the slightest bit slow, rather than energized, the latter being his usual state.

This was why he'd almost missed them. Missed the two boys, barely in their teens, running as if one of those zombie creatures was after them.

What caught Chris's attention, other than the fact that the teens were all but flying, was that the two looked paler than vanilla ice cream buried beneath a three-day snowfall.

Intrigued and definitely curious, Chris stopped going over just what had gone wrong with his fail-safe strategy last night, and became instantly alert and focused on what was happening right now.

It was a little after six in the morning and the sun had already staked out its position in the sky, so Chris knew his eyes weren't playing tricks on him. That his mind wasn't doing creative things with the night's leftover shadows. There *were* no shadows, only two teenage boys running from a strip mall as if their very lives depended on just how far away they could get and how fast they could do it.

Braking abruptly—and silently grateful that there was no one behind him—Chris did a creative U-turn and drove into the strip mall, instantly going in the same direction the boys were running—or fleeing, if that turned out to be the case. Part of his gut instincts—inherited from a family tree enormously populated by law enforcement agents—told him that "fleeing" was the more likely description.

Within a heartbeat, Chris brought his vehicle to a screeching halt right in front of the taller of the two teenagers. The youth fell, then quickly scrambled back up to his feet.

Fear and confusion were in both teens' eyes.

They stared at him, not like deer caught in the headlights of an oncoming car, but like two deer that had seen something really, really awful.

Chris rolled down the window closest to the teens. "Something wrong, boys?"

Neither answered him, not because they were trying to be evasive or difficult, but because neither one of them seemed able to speak. They were both struggling to catch their breath, their lungs all but bursting from their effort to put as much distance between themselves and whatever it was that they had either seen or encountered within the empty department store.

Making a judgment call, Chris turned off his engine and got out of his vehicle.

His eyes swept over the two teens, making a quick evaluation of any potential threat they might pose. This was Aurora, CA, deemed to be a normally safe city. But no place was perfect, and as his mother, Maeve, was fond of saying, even paradise had its serpent, as Adam and Eve sadly discovered.

Shorter and of slighter build than he was, the

two teens didn't seem to pose any sort of a threat. Wearing light windbreakers that had flapped wildly as they ran, the duo didn't look to be carrying any weapons, either, concealed or otherwise.

"Take your time," Chris told them patiently. "Catch your breath and then tell me what has you both so spooked."

Still gasping, the shorter one pointed frantically behind him to the building he and his friend had just vacated like two fledgling bats out of hell.

Chris took the opportunity to attempt to fill in some of the blanks and coax the story out of the breathless, frightened teens.

"Kresky's," he said, identifying their point of exit.

The duo nodded vigorously in response, but still didn't seem to be able to form any actual words.

In its day, Kresky's had been an upper-end department store, a chain of shops owned and developed by a wealthy East Coast-based family more than eighty years ago. At its zenith, the stores were located in major cities in almost every state in the country. They offered everything from clothing to cookware to toys. Prices were reasonable and customers were plentiful—until they weren't.

Once it stopped being *the* place where everyone shopped, the stores grew fewer in number until there were almost none left at all. The one in Aurora was among the last to give up the ghost and had just recently—four months ago, if Chris recalled correctly—held its going-out-of-business sale, before permanently closing its doors.

"What about Kresky's?" Chris asked, following that question with another one. "And what were you two doing in the store? It's been cleared out for months. Why would you want to break in?"

As far as he knew, that final sale had included virtually everything in the place, including the fixtures. Only the plumbing and the walls were left, a sad testimony to a once thriving store where he had accompanied Sally Howe, the love of his life his last year in high school, to pick out her senior prom dress.

Neither teen in front of him seemed to have sucked enough air into his lungs to attempt to explain why they would break into an abandoned department store. Instead, the taller of them had only two words, barely audible, to offer.

The moment Chris heard them, he realized that he wasn't being told why they had entered the building, but why they had exited it in such a huge hurry and why their complexions had turned so pasty white in the process.

"Dead body!"

Chapter 1

Sean Cavanaugh was accustomed to being the first one in the crime lab each morning. As the day shift crime scene lab manager, he liked getting a jump start on the day, as well as any work that might have been left over from the night before.

He had a top-notch, highly skilled crew that needed no hand-holding or close overseeing, beyond what might have been deemed necessary from a general organizational standpoint.

However, he could no longer lay claim to being the first one in each morning, not since his newest crime scene investigator had transferred in from out of state a little over nine months ago. Susannah Quinn, affectionately referred to by the people who worked with her as Suzie Q, seemed to always be somewhere on the premises no matter what the hour. She came in before anyone else, and no matter how late Sean stayed, she frequently stayed even longer. She also pulled double shifts on occasion and thought nothing of covering for her fellow CSI agents if they called in sick or took an unexpected vacation day.

The fact that she didn't rust in the occasional California rain was just about the only thing that convinced Sean the newest addition to the team wasn't a robot.

Walking into the lab on the way to his office, Sean, father of seven, uncle of countless more, many of whom were on the Aurora police force, stopped by Suzie's work area and set down a large covered cup of coffee he had picked up on his way in to work.

"Good morning. What's this?" she asked her superior, nodding at the container.

He'd picked up a smaller container of black coffee for himself. Sean liked his coffee the way he preferred his cases: simple. Young people, he'd discovered, liked creative coffee.

"I'm told it's the latest in fad coffee," he told her.

"And you bought it for me?" Suzie asked uncertainly.

Was he doing it in order to soften a blow? she couldn't help wondering. She'd come to like Sean Cavanaugh a great deal, since taking this position at the crime lab, but she had paid a painful price to learn to take nothing—and no one—at face value.

Sean nodded. "I knew you'd be here." After removing the lid from his own coffee, he paused to take a sip of the black liquid, savoring the heat as it wound through his veins and kick-started his system. "You know, Suzie," he went on, snapping the lid back on the container, "indentured servitude was abolished in this country about four centuries ago. People who get paid for what they do for a living get to keep regular hours—at least most of the time. That means—in most cases—they come in at a reasonable hour in the morning and then go home at a reasonable hour at night."

She smiled at him. It was a sunny smile that lit up a room and was meant to put whoever was speaking to her at ease. For the most part, it did, but every so often Sean had a feeling there was something behind the smile that no one was supposed to see. A secret that only Suzie was privy to.

Since he was a firm believer in other people's privacy, Sean made no effort to push through the barriers. He did, however, do what he could to make it clear to Suzie that if she ever needed to talk about anything—and that included subjects that had nothing whatsoever to do with work—she could always talk to him.

"I know that," she responded cheerfully. Reaching into the bottom drawer of her desk, she pulled out the small messenger bag she kept there. Taking out her wallet, she asked, "What do I owe you for the coffee?"

"How about you go home early for a change and we'll call it even?" Sean suggested.

It wasn't a deal Suzie felt she could honor. She shook her head, sending her straight hair swinging.

"That's okay. I don't mind staying longer if the job calls for it," she replied. "Besides, I wouldn't know what to do with myself if I left early."

She thought Sean would drop the subject there, but she thought wrong. He actually had a list of suggestions ready for her. "You could get a hobby, get a pet, catch a movie, enroll in a cooking class, learn to windsurf." The smile on his lips was nothing if not encouraging as he paused before adding, "The possibilities are endless."

One by one Suzie addressed his points matter-of-factly. "My hobby is crime solving. With the hours I keep, I wouldn't leave a pet alone all day—it wouldn't be fair. There's nothing currently playing in the movie theaters that I want to see. And FYI, I already know how to cook and windsurf," she concluded. "Besides, I like my job, so why shouldn't I put in some extra hours every now and then?"

Sean bit his tongue to keep from pointing out that it was a lot more than "every now and then." It seemed she put in extra hours every day.

"You have an answer for everything, don't you?" he said with a laugh.

Suzie was careful when she made her response. She didn't want Sean thinking of her as being argumentative. "At least for the points you raised."

Sean looked at the young woman thoughtfully. The way Suzie had worded her reply made him think that there was something she didn't have an answer to, something she wasn't willing to talk about. He was tempted to ask if he was right, but again, that would be prying, and if she wanted him to know more than what she'd said, she would have told him.

The woman was a puzzle, no doubt about it. But puzzles took time to solve. Time and patience. Fortunately, he had both.

"Then I'll leave you to those reports." He started to leave, but then paused to add one more thing. "You do realize that you're probably the only one of my people who willingly sits down to face reports without being hounded and threatened to do it."

That in itself had him wondering about her. Susannah Quinn was young, beautiful and smart. Surely she had to have a life beyond these four walls and the crime scenes she investigated.

But from all indications, as far as he could see, she didn't. There were no pictures on her desk, no mention of family or friends. There wasn't even a next-of-kin or the name of someone to notify in case of an emergency on her work application.

Why?

Suzie turned his comparison over in her head. "Paperwork isn't exactly something people really aspire to do."

"But you do it," Sean pointed out.

To her, paperwork was something to do to stave off going home and being alone with her thoughts. With her memories.

But she couldn't tell Sean this.

So she shrugged. "It's part of the job."

Sean laughed as he walked away. “I’m going to ask Brian if there’s any money to be found in the budget so I can have you cloned.”

Brian Cavanaugh was his brother and Aurora’s chief of detectives. As such he was far more into the budget end of the police department than Sean was.

“Until then, I’ll just work faster,” Suzie promised, getting back to the report again.

Sean stopped just short of the doorway. “Don’t you dare. There’s such a thing as working yourself to death and you’ll do none of us any good—least of all yourself—if you do that. I’m serious, Suzie,” he told her, his voice dropping an octave. “I want you to go home at least at a regular time if not earlier today.”

Suzie made a noise in response that told him she had heard his voice, but hadn’t heard the words or the gist of what he was saying.

This wasn’t over, Sean promised himself. And then he laughed under his breath. He knew a lot of managers who would love being in his place, love having an employee who never seemed to get enough of work and always seemed to be tirelessly on the job.

But as a father, he just didn’t think that kind of behavior was healthy. If nothing else, Suzie was too tunnel-visioned. Suzie Quinn needed to have balance in her life. She was far too young to be strictly all about work, especially since she gave him the impression that she wasn’t doing it to get ahead. If he had to make a guess, he would have said she was doing it for the sake of justice.

It made him wonder if Suzie was hiding from

something. Or more to the point, if there was something she was running from.

If things continued this way, Sean told himself as he walked into his office, he would have to do a little digging.

Suzie listened for the sound of a door closing. When she heard it, she released the breath she'd been holding and relaxed a little. She knew that her boss meant well when he tried to urge her to go home early, but he just didn't understand. There was no reason for her to do so because there was no one and nothing waiting for her. No anticipated mail in her mailbox, no long-awaited email on her computer, no texts or messages of any sort from anyone she wanted to hear from.

Suzie heard from her brother, Lane, only on the occasional holiday—and not always then. Her mother was no longer among the living, but her father still was. However, she had absolutely no desire to hear from the senior member of her now defunct family. So there was nothing and no one to fill her off-hours.

Oh, a sense of curiosity mixed with desperation had made her actually give in and attempt to do something outside work, but that experiment, undertaken yesterday, had fallen rather flat, so there was no point in revisiting it.

All it had accomplished was making her come to terms with the fact that she wasn't cut out for anything beyond work. She just wished that everyone else would come to the same conclusion and allow her to get on with her life the way she saw fit.

The immediate problem was that right now there was no case to occupy her mind or her skills, which was why, to fill the time, Suzie was doing the paperwork she had put off. It wasn't that she was more conscientious than most of the people who worked in the crime lab. She just didn't want to be alone with her thoughts. At least not yet. Not until she learned how to herd them all into a cage and keep them there, away from the day-to-day fabric of her life.

Aurora's criminal element, such as it was, wasn't cooperating. Although she would have been the first to admit that a crime-free city was a wonderful thing, Suzie couldn't help hoping that something would come up by the time she put the last of the stack of paperwork to bed.

More than anything, she really didn't want to be left to her own devices.

It wasn't all that long ago that Chris had been the exact same age as the boys he'd just cornered. What he couldn't remember, though, was ever being as scared as they appeared to be.

At the moment, he was having a difficult time getting either one to be coherent, even after they had recovered their breaths and voices. Now the problem seemed to be that they were both talking over one another. The end result was an annoying cacophony that left him as unenlightened as he had been when he'd first cornered them.

Straining to follow both disjointed monologues, Chris finally gave up trying to make heads or tails out of the dissonance. He drew in a breath, whistled long and loud, until both teenagers finally stopped talking at the speed of a runaway freight train.

Stunned, they stared at the man who had pulled them over.

"Don't you want to hear what happened?" they cried in unison. It was the first time since they'd come flying out of the building that they were both intelligible.

"More than you can possibly know," Chris assured them, "but I won't find anything out if you keep on talking over one another like two screech owls in a barnyard competition. You," he said, randomly picking the taller of the two. "What's your name?"

"Bill," the teen answered nervously, apparently worried that he was being singled out. "Bill Peterson."

"And I'm—" The other teenager began to give his name, but Chris held up his hand.

"You'll have your turn. Okay, Bill Peterson," he said, addressing the first teenager. "Why were you and your friend here flying out of the old Kresky building like the devil himself was after you?"

The question had the teenagers turning ghostly pale again. Bill cleared his throat before speaking. "You're not going to believe me."

"Try me," Chris said patiently, giving the impression that he wasn't about to go anywhere until he got the truth out of them.

The two teenagers exchanged looks.

"Look at me, Bill," he ordered. "Look at me when you answer."

Bill flushed. "Maybe we better show you," he muttered.

Instead of urging them on, Chris glanced from one to the other. He figured it was time to get the second teen's name just in case the two got it into their heads to take off again. If they went in different directions, he could go after only one. Having both their names—if they weren't lying—at least gave him a fighting chance of bringing the teenagers in.

He had a feeling this wasn't just some prank. Something definitely was going on.

"And your name is?" His no-nonsense stare seemed to glue the second teen's feet to the ground.

"Allen, sir." The youth actually swallowed. Any second, Chris expected to see his Adam's apple dance. "Allen Kott."

"Okay, Allen Kott, why don't you and Bill here show me what got the two of you looking paler than Snow White." When the duo looked as if they intended to walk back into the building behind him, Chris gestured that they were to lead the way. He wanted to keep an eye on them the whole time.

The teens complied.

"How did you two happen to be in the building?" Chris asked casually as they crossed to the abandoned department store. "It's supposed to be locked up."

Bill laughed nervously. "Yeah, supposed to be."

"But it wasn't," Chris assumed. This was prime real estate. Most of the strip malls and stores in the city were. He couldn't see the building being left haphazardly opened so that anyone could have access to it. A great deal of destruction could be done in a minimum of time. That could generate a costly problem for anyone who'd just bought the property. "Did you break in?"

"No, it was already open," Allen told him. "I swear," he quickly added.

Chris was still having a hard time buying that. "How did you know?" he asked. "Or did you just keep trying different doors until you got lucky?"

"We figured we'd find it open because this was where the big bash was last night," Allen told him matter-of-factly.

"What big bash?" Chris asked.

Were they pulling his leg, after all? But there was no mistaking the look of fear he'd seen. That had been very real and there had to be a cause behind it. How did it connect to this so-called "big bash" they were talking about?

"The *big* one." When Chris gave no indication that he was any clearer on the subject than he had been a moment ago, Allen stressed, "The *floating* one."

"A *floating* big bash," Chris repeated. It still wasn't making any sense to him.

"Yeah, man," Bill said almost impatiently. "These rich guys, they find these big, empty venues to hold these big, flashy parties. Lots of food, lots of dancing, lots of really gorgeous women in expensive clothes with expensive jewelry. None of this fake stuff, you know?" he asked, as if trying to make himself clear. "Everything about these women is super-real."

Chris stopped walking, his suspicions aroused. "And you know this how?"

"We've seen them," Bill said. Allen hit him in the ribs with his elbow. "What's that for?" he demanded.

The answer to that was evident by the way Chris looked at the teens. "You've been to these parties?"

"Not exactly," Bill said, with far less bravado. "We kinda hid out and watched them all go in."

Chris looked from one teen to the other, waiting. "Go on."

Allen picked up the thread as they began walking again. "When it was over and everyone left, we thought we'd go in and, you know, scout around. See if anybody left anything behind, like maybe dropped some money or some jewelry we could sell." He looked to see if the detective understood what he was saying. "We weren't stealing or nothing."

Chris used a more descriptive word. "You were scavenging."

"We were hunters," Bill said, with just a touch of indignation, attempting to glide right over the fact that they were both trespassing on what was at bottom private property.

For now, Chris went along with the euphemism. "Okay, and exactly what was it that you two big game hunters found?"

The teens' bravado was gone again, vanishing like the first blush of spring beneath a sun grown too hot too fast.

And then Chris saw why.

They were inside the deserted department store now, and rather than finding the debris that was usually left behind after a building was all but gutted, Chris saw glitter strewn across the floor like the confetti left after a parade.

And over in the corner, hidden behind a long table that had been brought in to accommodate food or a VJ or something along those lines, was the unclad body of a young woman whose color had been drained out of her less than a day ago.

Chapter 2

Taking out his flashlight, Chris crossed over to the body quickly. While there was some light coming in through the store windows, they were far enough away to make visibility around the body rather dim.

Chris panned around the area slowly. The dead woman appeared to be a blonde in her midtwenties. There was nothing to distinguish her from any of the hundreds of other hopeful, beautiful blondes who flocked to Southern California each year, their heads full of dreams, searching for fame and fortune.

This blonde's search had been traumatically and permanently terminated, Chris thought, wondering who she was and how many lives were going to be affected by her death.

He squatted down to get a closer look at the immediate crime scene, searching for anything that could give him a glimmer of insight as to why she'd been killed and why she'd been left like this.

Behind him, the two teenagers who had led him here were becoming antsy. He glanced over his shoulder to make sure they weren't getting ready to flee.

"She was like that when we found her, honest," Allen cried the second Chris made eye contact with him.

Bill added his agitated voice to his friend's testimony. "We didn't do anything to her!"

Because of the lack of blood in the immediate area, Chris assumed that the woman had been killed somewhere else and then moved.

The question now was who moved her, the killer or these agitated teenagers. Turning off his flashlight, Chris got back up to his feet and faced them. "Did either one of you touch her?" he asked.

"You mean, like when she was dead?" Allen cried, his brown eyes widening. The idea clearly horrified him. "Hell, no!" he declared emphatically. "She's *dead*."

Chris turned to the other teen, waiting for his answer. Bill looked as if he was in danger of swallowing his own tongue—or throwing up. He shook his head vigorously. When he finally regained his ability to talk, he said, "We got out of here as soon as we saw her. We're not freaks." Stunned by the suggestion Chris had made, he cried, "Hey, man, what kind of people do you know?"

"Not the kind that you would invite to a party," Chris murmured. Taking out his phone, he started to put in a call to his precinct. But he stopped when he saw that the teens were about to leave. "Where do you think you two are going?"

Bill and Allen exchanged looks. "We got class," Bill told him, as if that was their get-out-of-jail-free card.

His call temporarily put on hold, Chris moved to block their exit. "Not right now, you don't."

Allen appeared distressed. "But I've got a second-period test," the teen complained, then all but wailed, "I can't miss it."

"I'll write you a note," Chris told him dismissively. "Stay put or I'll have to cuff you." He didn't trust them to obey. "Now stand over there where I can watch you," he instructed, indicating the wall right behind the dead woman who had sent them running.

The teens regarded the body nervously.

"Could we stand over here instead, not so close to her?" Allen asked, pointing to an area in the opposite direction.

"Death isn't catching," Chris informed him in a no-nonsense voice. "Unless, of course, you and your friend try to run."

Pinning them with a look that all but nailed the two teens to the spot, Chris completed his call to the precinct and started the ball rolling.

Dispatched by Sean Cavanaugh, Dirk Bogart peered into the lab, looking for the woman he'd been told by his boss to fetch.

Spotting her at the far end of the room, Bogart smiled as he called out, "Put your papers aside, Suzie Q. We've got a live one. Or rather," he corrected with a grin that went from ear to ear, "a dead one. Boss man says to tell you that you're up. I'll drive."

The words came out like rapid gunfire, one after another, barely allowing Suzie to absorb one sentence before Bogart had already moved on to the third.

Replaying the words a beat or so behind their actual lightning-fast delivery, Suzie nodded and grabbed the gear she personally packed and then repacked after each trip to a crime scene. Experience had taught her that anything else would already be in the car and ready to go.

Because she liked being in control of any situation she found herself in, Suzie preferred driving to the crime scene and she preferred to do that driving alone. But she knew that making waves, even little waves, put people off, and in this case she had to admit it really wasn't worth it. She was careful to pick her battles and fought only those that really needed to be fought.

This was not one of them.

Although, she thought several minutes into the drive, she would have done a lot better on her own. If there was anything that Dirk liked better than the sound of his own voice, Suzie had a feeling it hadn't been discovered yet.

The two-year CSI vet talked the entire way to the crime scene. He talked about the weather, the state of the country and how he was a thrill junky, which was why, he went on to tell her, he'd taken this job in the first place.

For the most part, Suzie managed to tune him out, and made appropriate noises that might have been taken as agreement only when it sounded as if he was ready to challenge her if she didn't concur with his many stated opinions.

When Bogart finally brought the vehicle to a stop at what was clearly a roped-off area, Suzie was quick to get out of the car, clutching her crime scene case to her. She was glad to see that Sean was already on the scene.

Spotting him, she made a beeline for the man.

"I see we managed to get you away from your paperwork," Sean observed pleasantly.

"Could we get me away from Bogart now, as well?"

The words just slipped out, surprising her as much as they obviously did Sean. Ordinarily, she wasn't given to complaining and she could see that her request immediately registered with the man.

He laughed, an understanding look on his face. "Couldn't stop talking, could he?"

Following her superior into the abandoned department store, Suzie shook her head. "Not for a second. I didn't know a human being was capable of saying that many words a minute."

Sean walked toward the taped-off area. "I thought that maybe being in your company, he'd pick up a few tips on how to be silent. Guess not," he concluded philosophically. "Next time, you can ride with me."

"I think I'd really like that." She tried to sound neutral about it, but didn't quite succeed. She heard the older man laugh again.

"He'll hit his stride, given enough time," Sean told her.

"What if that *is* his stride?" Suzie asked, far from comfortable with that thought.

"People transfer out of the department on occasion," Sean answered, as if that was something that might give her hope. "The crime scene is right over there." He pointed ahead of them.

Relieved that Bogart hadn't caught up to them with the rest of the equipment yet, Suzie hurried closer to Sean.

"Do we know anything yet?" she asked, assuming that whoever had called the crime into their division had given a few details.

"Only that apparently Aurora has a whole nightlife I know nothing about," said a man who walked up behind them. "According to the two kids who found the body, there are supposedly decadent 'floating' parties being thrown in abandoned, high-end buildings all through Southern California."

Sean nodded, taking the scene in. "Anything else, Chris?"

"I was hoping you could tell me," the newcomer replied. That was when his voice finally struck a familiar chord for her and Suzie turned around.

About to say something else to his uncle, Chris

could only stare at the young woman who had come in with Sean. Recognition came, riding a thunderbolt, in less than a heartbeat.

The woman from last night's party.

The one he hadn't been able to get to first base with.

First base? Hell, he didn't even get to pick up the bat to begin to play the game. Their entire interaction had consisted of a great many back-and-forth exchanges that had passed as banter, at least to his ear. Looking back, he realized that it might not have necessarily seemed that way to her.

As a matter of fact, since she had disappeared the way she had, he was sure of it.

Yet here she was, standing in front of him, looking very different in the light of day—and yet enticingly the same, except that she was wearing jeans and a jacket instead of the clinging cocktail dress she'd worn last night.

"You," Chris stated.

A great deal was inferred in that single word. It spoke of the party she'd attended and the time he'd spent attempting to get to know her. It spoke of his bewilderment when he'd turned away just for a moment, only to find her gone. He'd scanned the area, trying to find her, before he finally gave up and moved on.

Moving on had ultimately proved more fruitful, which was why he was so tired this morning.

Tired, but far from satisfied.

He had to get it into his head that he wasn't eighteen anymore, Chris told himself, and that any all-nighters he pulled had to be centered around work, not partying.

"Me," Suzie replied with a smile, neither her expression nor her voice giving anything away.

For all Chris knew, it could be just an automatic response. Except that it *was* her, the woman who had, like a very old song had once said, drawn him from across a crowded room. He was sure of it.

Sean looked from his nephew to the young woman he felt had all the earmarks of becoming his best investigator, once whatever baggage she was secretly carrying was unpacked and put away. "You two know one another?" he asked, interested. It certainly sounded that way to him.

Chris was the first to speak up. "Apparently not," he admitted, thinking of the way last night had gone and the vanishing act she had pulled. He'd waited around before ultimately moving on, but his mystery woman never made a reappearance. He'd just assumed she had left the club. "But not for lack of trying," he added significantly, still looking at the woman who had come in with his uncle. From the way she was dressed, she was obviously part of the department. Something else that hadn't come up last night.

Rather than being annoyed or feeling as if he had been played, Chris found himself intrigued.

"Then let me introduce you," Sean proposed, looking from his nephew to the young investigator as he quickly assessed the situation. He'd been exposed to enough younger Cavanaugh males and their robust hormones when it came to dealings with the opposite sex to pick up on what was going on—and what possibly hadn't, as well.

"Chris, this is Suzie Quinn, the newest crime scene investigator on my team. She's a lot sharper than her very youthful appearance might lead you to believe," he assured his nephew—or maybe it was more like a warning. "Nothing gets by her," Sean said proudly. "Suzie, this is Detective Christian Cavanaugh O'Bannon, one of my nephews. One of my *many* nephews," he added with a laugh.

She knew there were more than a few Cavanaughs scattered throughout the various departments of the Aurora Police Department, but up until now, she had to admit she hadn't really paid all that much attention to the fact. It wasn't something that seemed work-related to her.

"How many nephews do you have?" she asked, turning her attention to her supervisor rather than the guy who had tried to make points with her on her one and only venture into a social scene in the last three years.

She'd learned her lesson there.

Sean's smile was almost rueful. "To be honest, I no longer know. Every time I turn around there seem to be more of them—nieces *and* nephews," he clarified. "We have a very prolific family tree."

"Apparently," Suzie murmured.

"However," Sean continued, turning his attention to the young woman whose death had brought them all here, "being prolific is something this poor individual will never get the chance to bc." He looked back at his nephew. "Do we know how she got here?"

"All we know at the moment is that according to those two kids—" Chris indicated the duo he had standing nearby "—there was something like a wild party here last night. I'm assuming that she attended that event, and somewhere during the evening or early hours, became a casualty."

"Did those two boys witness anything?" Sean asked.

Chris laughed shortly. "According to them, everything and nothing. All I could get out of them was that they fell asleep waiting for the party to be over. When they woke up, everyone was long gone. They went into the building—which they claimed was unlocked—to see if they could find anything of value that the partygoers might have left behind."

Sean saw that Suzie had moved closer to the dead woman and crouched down, studying her intently.

"She looks like she might have been valuable to someone," she murmured, more to herself than to either of the two men next to her.

"Why don't you try to talk to those two boys, Suzie?" Sean suggested when she rose to her feet again. "See if you can get anything more out of them than they told Chris."

Although generally mild mannered and easygoing, Chris reacted to what he felt his uncle wasn't saying aloud, but was inferring: that he had done less than a good job with the teens.

"I didn't exactly use a rubber hose on them, Sean," he protested. "I was my usual charming, persuasive self."

"Then it's a wonder those poor guys aren't traumatized," Suzie said wryly as she went to interview the two boys.

Torn between going with her just to see if she could do better with the duo, and hanging back to ask his uncle a few questions about the woman, Chris decided to go with the latter, but only for a few moments.

He had to admit that he was still feeling his way around in this brand-new family hierarchy. There were some people within the department who were less charitable. They referred to the Cavanaughs as a dynasty—and not in a kind way.

To Chris, the fact that he had so many relatives in the police department just made it the family business. A great many family members followed one another into a line of work. For his, that involved all different walks of law enforcement. That there were so many of them didn't change the fact that they were still, at heart, a family. And as such, they shared things. Like information.

The information he required was of a very specific nature.

"How long has Suzie been working for you?" Chris asked as he followed his uncle.

Sean began to process the crime scene. Bogart had finally entered and was setting up the equipment he'd carried in.

"Nine months," Sean replied.

That seemed like a short amount of time. Chris couldn't help wondering where she'd worked before that, and asked.

"She wasn't working for me." Sean glanced up at him and smiled. "Arizona. Same field," he added, before his nephew could ask. Obviously there was something about Suzie that Chris found intriguing. It wasn't hard to see why. Sean had noticed that Dirk had been dancing around her, showing off like an eager puppy. To her credit, Suzie appeared to be oblivious to all of this. "Anything else?"

He might as well go for broke. "Is she married?" Chris asked bluntly.

Sean paused and looked at his nephew for a long moment. He didn't want to see either of them getting hurt. "Don't go getting ideas about this one, Chris."

Chris came to the only conclusion he could. "Then she's married."

"I didn't say that."

He circled around to get in front of his uncle. "What *are* you saying?" he asked.

Sean thought of the impression he'd gotten more than once when he'd talked with Suzie. "That some people need to work things out before they can come out and play."

Chris wasn't sure he understood. "What kind of things?"

"Things they don't broadcast." Suzie's issues were her own. Sean wasn't about to intrude or second-guess what was going on in the young woman's head.

"She's very good at her job, Chris. I don't want to lose her."

"Don't worry," he replied, flashing a confident grin. "I have no intention of making her go away, Uncle Sean." Chris reverted to the more familiar form of address, since they were alone. "In fact," he said, walking off to see how Suzie's interview with the teens was going, "it's the exact opposite."

"Just remember that I have your mother on speed dial," Sean called after him.

Blowing out a breath, Sean shook his head. He supposed, if he thought long enough, he could remember being that young and feeling that invincible once. But right now, it seemed an eternity ago.

Maybe two eternities.

Sean roused himself. He had a crime scene to get back to and assess. And a young woman to avenge. Everything else had to take second place.

"Ah, Dirk," he said, beckoning Bogart forward. "Just in time."

He pretended not to notice the disappointment on the investigator's face as he kept the young man from joining Suzie.

Chapter 3

It was totally unexpected. Striding across the former department store toward Suzie, Chris was just in time to see it.

To see her smile.

She turned around just as he reached her, and the smile on her lips was nothing short of dazzling. It actually seemed to light up the area.

"Wait right there, boys," Suzie said as she left the two teens and joined him. "Detective O'Bannon will probably want to talk to you before he lets you leave."

Reaching the crime scene investigator, Chris turned his back to the teenagers so that they weren't able to overhear his conversation with her. He couldn't help noticing that she seemed exceptionally pleased with herself. It piqued his curiosity.

"You've made yourself at home with my witnesses," he noted.

"Crime scene witnesses," Suzie corrected. "And I think I've got everything that you might want."

He couldn't contain the grin that curved his lips. "No question about that."

Suzie's eyes narrowed, telling him she didn't find him witty, nor was she flattered. "I was talking about the crime scene."

"Okay, we'll go with that for now," Chris agreed. "And what is it you've got that I wasn't able to get?" he challenged gamely.

Suzie deliberately started small. "I have their names and addresses—"

He waved dismissively. "Already got that," he told her.

She hated being cut off like this. He could have the decency to hear her out. "I wasn't finished," she informed him.

Chris inclined his head as if to tender an apology. "Sorry, go ahead."

"I have their names and addresses," she repeated, "so that we can send them their cell phones once our computer technician takes a look at them."

He thought of the mind-numbing selfies that were probably on both cell phones. "And she'd want to do that because?"

Obviously, she was going to have to spell this all out for him, Suzie thought. The preening homicide detective wasn't quite as brilliant as he thought himself to be. "Because our teen voyeurs and would-be enterprising thieves might not have gotten into the party while it was going on, but they were tenacious enough to find a window that wasn't covered, and they took videos of the people attending. It might amount to nothing," she said, "but then again..."

"It might be something," Chris agreed, instantly hopping on her bandwagon. He looked over her shoulder at the teens waiting to be released, and frowned. "They didn't tell me they took videos of the party attendees with their phones."

The look on Suzie's face said he should have figured that part out for himself because it was so obvious. "They're teenagers with smart phones. They take videos of *everything* at this age."

Rather than appearing annoyed the way she'd expected him to, there was admiration in the detective's eyes. It took her aback.

"You're good," he told her.

He expected her to preen a little, because it was her due, given the circumstances. But she wound up surprising him by merely shrugging her shoulders. "Just doing my job."

In his opinion, what she'd just done could make his job a whole lot easier. "If we didn't have an audience, I'd kiss you," he declared, looking at the two cell phones she produced. She was holding them gingerly with a handkerchief.

"Then lucky for you we have an audience, because otherwise I'd be forced to deck you," Suzie responded, offering him a spasmodic smile at the end of her statement.

The corners of her mouth went down again as she became serious. Sealing each phone, one at a time, into an evidence bag, Suzie carefully wrote down the time, date and which youth it belonged to.

Finished, she held the transparent bags out to Chris. "Drop these off with the lab tech after you take these boys to their school."

Rather than grow irritated that the woman he had tried and failed to pick up last night was issuing orders to him, Chris took it all in stride. "You do have a take-charge personality, don't you?"

Suzie waited for him to challenge her. When he didn't, she said simply, "Again, just doing what needs to be done."

Chris was about to say something further to her but she turned away, shifting her attention to the next thing on the list: taking close-ups of the dead woman, as well as the area around her. The victim might not have been killed in this exact place, but there could be some sort of clue accidentally left behind that would lead them to identify where the woman *had* been murdered.

Chris knew when he was being dismissed. For now, because he wanted to get the cell phones logged into evidence and then to the computer lab as soon as possible, he let it go.

"C'mon, guys. Teacher's issuing you a hall pass," he told the two teenagers. "Looks like you'll be going to school, after all."

Allen and his friend exchanged glances as they were being herded out of the former department store. Bill nodded in response to Allen's unspoken question. Two minds with a single thought: ditching school.

"Hey, if it's all the same to you, can you just drop us off at the Golden Gate Plaza?" Allen asked, referring to the largest shopping mall in Aurora.

"During school hours?" Chris asked, dramatically putting his hand to his chest. "Now what kind of an officer of the law would I be if I aided and abetted your hooky playing?" he asked. "You're going to school, boys," he told them cheerfully. "And I'm taking you there."

The duo grumbled quietly—until they reached Chris's car, a Lincoln Continental from a by-gone era when fins still meant something. The car was large, and provided the protection of a tank.

"Hey, is this *yours*?" Bill asked, as he and Allen stopped next to the vehicle Chris had brought them to.

Chris looked at the duo as if he was dealing with a pair of living brain donors. "No, when I saw you two running, I stole someone else's ride so I could cut you off in an impressive car. Of course this is mine," he said in irritation as he unlocked the doors.

Neither teenager seemed to be insulted by the sarcastic response. Allen ran his hand along the panel closest to him. "I guess I didn't notice what an outstanding piece of craftsmanship this was."

Chris noted that the teen was all but drooling on his car. He anticipated the next question that either boy was going to ask and headed it off. "I got the car by saving up every spare dime and working really, really hard. I think that the two of you should stop fixating on my ride and start figuring out what you're going to tell your parents."

Bill looked at him as if he had just begun speaking in a foreign language that the teenager couldn't quite grasp. "Our parents?"

Digging deep, Chris searched for even simpler words to use as he explained. "Well, yeah, because after I drop you off, I'm going to make it a point to pay a visit to your parents. I think they're entitled to know how you're spending your school nights."

"Yesterday wasn't a school night," Bill protested. "It was a Sunday."

The teen wasn't following him, Chris thought. Definitely not the shiniest apple on the tree. "But today's a school day, isn't it?"

Bill still didn't look as if he understood where this was going. "Huh?"

Chris shook his head as he turned into the high school parking lot. "See, if you studied more and lurked less, you'd understand what I'm talking about. Look sharp, guys," he told them, pointing to the building on the right. "School's up ahead."

It grew very quiet in his car as he pulled into a parking space that had a time limit of twenty minutes printed right above it.

"Can you put a rush on it?" Chris asked the slender, pretty computer technician less than half an hour after depositing the teenagers at the school.

Valri Cavanaugh frowned ever so slightly as she looked down at the two bagged cell phones that had just been placed on her desk. Raising her eyes to her cousin's, she said, "You do realize that just because your middle name is Cavanaugh doesn't mean you automatically go to the head of the line, right?"

"Right," he agreed, then went on to enumerate the reasons he felt he could ask his cousin to put a rush on lifting videos from the two phones. "This goes to the head of the line because it might show us who killed a perfectly innocent young woman who looked enough like you to be your sister. Because the teenaged boys who own these devices are even now having withdrawal symptoms, enduring traumatic separations from their cell phones, and we all know they would have rather given up a kidney. And last but not least, because I'm trying to impress this really cute crime scene investigator with my crime solving powers." Finished, he took in a deep breath, then said, "For all the above reasons, I need you and your really clever expertise to lift and enhance the videos on these phones"

This was not Valri's first rodeo—nor was it her first sweet-talking relative. Growing up with her brothers had made her all but immune to this sort of charismatic persuasion. "What you need, Detective O'Bannon," she informed him, "is help."

Chris was all innocence as he replied, "That's what I'm asking for."

Valri wouldn't budge. "Really serious help."

"Still on the same page," Chris told her.

"Serious *mental* help, Christian," she emphasized, feeling as if she still wasn't getting through to him.

"Haven't had your morning tea yet, have you?" Chris asked sympathetically. He knew that his cousin was partial to tea, unlike the rest of his clan, who all but ran on black coffee.

"Haven't had my breakfast yet," Valri complained in a weak moment. "I came in early to try to catch up on my backlog."

And that was clearly not happening, she thought, looking accusingly at the sealed cell phones on her desk. It was just a matter of time before she gave in and she knew it.

"Well, if you do this—" he nodded at the evidence bags "—it'll be that much less backlog you'll have to deal with."

Valri blew out a breath. She'd made a valiant attempt, but now had to give up. The less time she spent resisting, the more she would have for the rest of her work.

"All right, I'll do it," she declared. "It'll be worth it just to get you out of my hair."

Chris sifted a long, silky blond strand through his fingers. "And such lovely hair it is, too."

Valri pulled the strand away from him. "You can cut the blarney, Chris. I already agreed to process the cell phones."

He pretended to look stunned. "Valri, I'm surprised at you. We don't avail ourselves of 'blarney.' That's for the Irish. Our ancestors came from Scotland."

Valri sighed. The man had a wonderful baritone

voice that made the most trivial information sound important. But even so, it was time to get him out of her lab.

"You know, the longer you talk," she told him, "the longer it's going to take for me to go through all this."

"Consider me gone," Chris announced, already heading for the door. "Oh, and don't forget to make copies of those party videos," he reminded her. "Uncle Sean's going to want to take a look at them himself. You know how hands-on he is."

"As opposed to being all handsy," Valri countered, looking at her cousin knowingly.

Rather than pretend not to understand what she was talking about, Chris grinned. "We all have our calling," he said, and then winked. "But between you and me, my hands never go anywhere they're not invited."

"Just go!" Valri ordered, pointing to the doorway with a laugh.

"Like I was never here," he replied and made himself scarce.

"Miss me?" Chris asked late that afternoon, stepping into Suzie's work area.

Lost in thought as she'd been, she stifled a gasp. The detective had caught her by surprise and it took an effort not to show it. Suzie didn't like revealing any sort of vulnerability, and to be caught off guard or unprepared was to be vulnerable, in her book.

Collecting herself, she answered with a careless,

"Not even for a second." Then suggested, "Try being gone longer."

"Maybe next time," he promised.

Although she wanted to ignore him, she couldn't. It wasn't just that his presence seemed to fill up the room, even one as large as the lab. He'd brought something with him, as well.

"What's that?" she asked, nodding at the tablet he had just dropped on her desk.

"That is your very own copy of Aurora's wild nightlife," he told her.

"I thought I was already looking at it," Suzie deadpanned.

Chris inclined his head. "Touché," he replied, then, playing along, said, "This is the video version. Or more specifically, a copy of what our very own wizard of a computer technician managed to get off the Three Stooges Minus One's cell phone videos of the so-called 'floating' party that they couldn't crash—thanks to you," he added, because, after all, if Suzie hadn't asked the right questions and found out about the videos the teenagers had made, they wouldn't have this potential lead.

"Nice save," Suzie allowed, amused despite herself. "But you don't have to worry about hurting my feelings if you don't mention my part in securing the videos. I'm not in this for the credit."

Chris leaned casually against her desk, every inch the consummate laid-back detective. "What are you in this for?" he asked.

She could feel his eyes pinning her down even if

she deliberately didn't look up and make eye contact. "A regular paycheck at the end of the week," she told him dismissively.

"Uh-uh," Chris said.

He leaned down in front of her, getting in her face and making it impossible for her to avoid eye contact with him. His gaze felt as if it could delve right into her soul and she really resented the invasion.

"That isn't it, either," he told her confidently.

"Then what is?" she asked, doing her best not to allow her temper to flare.

Suzie braced herself to listen to the detective spin his outlandish theories. At the very least, she expected to hear him spout some grandiose rhetoric. But it was her turn to be surprised by him.

"I don't know yet," Chris told her honestly. "But I'm working on it. I'll let you know when I come up with an answer."

Suzie frowned. She didn't have time to waste watching this too-handsome-for-his-own-good detective trying to mesmerize her. She had work to do and so did he.

"Your time would be better spent coming up with answers regarding our dead woman," she said in a no-nonsense tone.

Our.

Her slip of the tongue was not lost on Chris. The grin on his lips told her so before he uttered a word. "Our first joint venture. We should savor this."

"What I'd savor," she informed him, "is some

peace and quiet so I can work. Specifically, some time away from you."

The expression that came over Chris's face was one of doubt. "Now, if we spend time apart, how are we going to work on this case together?" he asked, conveying that what she'd just said lacked logic.

Suzie had only one word to give him in response to his question. "Productively."

With that, she went back to doing her work, but that lasted for only a few moments. A minute at best. Though she tried to block out his presence, he still managed to get to her.

He was standing exactly where he had been, watching her so intently that she could literally feel his eyes on her skin. It caused her powers of concentration to deteriorate until they finally became nonexistent.

Unable to stand it, she looked up and glared at him. "What do you want, O'Bannon?" she muttered. It took everything she had not to shout the question at him. The man was making her crazy.

Chris never hesitated as he answered her. "Dinner."

She clenched her jaw. "You can buy it in any supermarket," she informed him coldly.

He sidestepped the roadblocks she was throwing up as if they weren't there.

"With you."

This time Suzie was the one who didn't hesitate for a second. "Not at any price. Now please go before I take out my manual on workplace harassment and start underlining passages to get you banned from my lab."

"It's the crime scene lab, not yours," he reminded her pleasantly, taking a page out of her book. And then Chris inclined his head. "Until the next time."

"There *is* no next time," she countered, steaming even though she refused to look up again.

"Don't forget we're working this case together," he told her cheerfully.

He thought he heard Suzie say "Damn" under her breath as he left the lab.

Chris smiled to himself.

Chapter 4

Suzie counted to a hundred.

Slowly.

She'd already gotten the impression that O'Bannon was the impatient type, so if he was planning on doubling back to make a reappearance in her lab, she was fairly certain he'd do it way before she reached a hundred.

Just to be sure, she counted to a hundred a second time.

Finished, she relaxed and turned her attention to the tablet the detective had deposited almost carelessly on her desk—as if he didn't know that her interest would immediately be drawn to it. She mentally crossed her fingers that the two fumbling teens had somehow managed to capture something of significance on their phones, and that it wasn't all just blurred videos.

Heaven knew she wasn't getting anywhere with the photos she'd taken at what now amounted to the secondary crime scene, Suzie thought. If the woman's killer had dumped her body there—and Suzie was certain that whoever it was had—she had no hope of singling out his or her shoe prints from all the other prints that were so pervasive around the body.

She hadn't found any traces of blood in the area, either. None belonging to the victim and none that might have pointed to her would-be killer. In addition, Suzie hadn't seen anything beneath the young woman's nails to indicate that she had tried to fight off her killer.

What she did find, however, was a great deal of spilled alcohol, all varieties, on the floor, as well as traces of drugs that at first assessment appeared to be of the recreational variety.

She found it rather ironic that she was dealing with that sort of party scene now. She herself had almost gone that route when the scandal had broken wide open. Only her fierce resolve to hold herself together for her mother's sake had kept her from doing it. Kept her from availing herself of the alcohol and drugs that would have numbed her acute pain, as well as her acute shame, and brought her peace, at least for a little while.

And then, after the trial was over, her mother had

killed herself, abruptly bringing what was left of Suzie's own shattered world crashing down on her.

She paused for a moment, drawing in a long breath as she struggled to center herself and put the barriers back up where they belonged. She needed to contain those memories, to keep them as far away from her mind as she possibly could.

Though she hated admitting to weakness, she knew that she couldn't handle those memories yet.

Maybe she never would.

Squaring her shoulders, she pulled the tablet closer and activated the video. She had clues to find and a murder to make sense of. She owed it to the dead girl.

She owed it to a lot of dead girls.

It felt like she'd been staring at the videos, playing them over and over again, for hours now. Each time she did, she picked up something new she hadn't seen before.

But now her eyes felt as if they were burning.

Leaning back in her chair for a moment, Suzie closed them.

When she opened her eyes again, only the extreme control that she had learned to exercise kept her from screaming. Even so, her heart pounded like a war drum.

When she'd shut her eyes to momentarily rest them, she'd been alone in the lab. When she opened them, she found she wasn't alone any longer.

Chris was standing right in front of her, less than two feet away.

Damn O'Bannon, he would wind up giving her a heart attack.

"Why are you sneaking up on me?" she demanded, unconsciously pressing her hand against her chest, as if to keep her heart from leaping out.

"I wasn't sneaking," Chris told her innocently. "Although I did leave my tap shoes at home. The chief of d's frowns on scuff marks the taps make on the wood," he explained, keeping an entirely straight face.

She didn't have the patience to listen to him go on and on. Her composure had faded hours ago.

"It's late, O'Bannon. What are you doing here?" she asked.

Rather than becoming defensive, he turned the tables on her, saying mildly, "I could ask you the same thing."

She didn't care for the nature of his question, or his attitude. She hadn't invaded his work space; he had invaded hers.

And she wanted him gone.

"I have work to do. I *like* working late," she emphasized. "There's usually no one around to bother me," she added, looking at him pointedly. Her message was clear.

Or so she thought.

Chris nodded. "I had a hunch," he told her. "That's why I came back."

Give the situation, he wasn't making any sense.

But then, she was beginning to think that he was doing that on purpose. Well, whatever his game was, she didn't have the time or the desire to play. She wanted him gone.

Now.

"Unless you have some new information for me—" Suzie began, but she never got the opportunity to finish.

"No, no new information," Chris confessed, making no move to leave.

"Well then—"

Again he didn't give her a chance to finish. "I do, however, have this."

She still had no idea what he was talking about—or why the man just couldn't take a hint, even if she was hitting him over the head with it.

"'This?'" she questioned.

She looked on in surprise as he hefted a large paper bag from the floor and placed it on her desk—obviously one he'd brought in when she had her eyes closed. Chris began to unpack its contents.

Within seconds, he'd taken out five steaming white containers, each embossed with red Chinese characters on the sides.

"You know the old saying, if the mountain won't come to Moh—"

"I am neither the mountain nor the person in your imaginary drama," Suzie pointed out sharply.

Chris rolled with the punches. "Okay, then let's just call it a mercy dinner." Since she didn't instantly protest, he continued. "You haven't moved from that spot since I dropped off the videos. You've got to be starving by now."

Suzie's mouth dropped open, but she recovered quickly. "You're spying on me?" she cried, not knowing if she should be creeped out or just angry. Who did this man think he was to take over this way? To keep tabs on her every movement?

"No," he stated. "What I did was have a casual conversation with my uncle." Before she could take him to task any further, he added, "I called him to let him know I'd gotten the cell phone videos copied and that I'd dropped them off with you. That's when he mentioned your habit of burning the midnight oil and that you'd probably be doing the same thing with this. He expressed concern that you had a habit of forgetting to eat."

Chris glanced at her pointedly as he flattened the now empty bag, setting it off to one side. He had put out the boxes, as well as the chopsticks and napkins that had come with the order. He also laid out the two sets of plastic cutlery he had specifically requested. He had no idea if Suzie knew how to use chopsticks, and he'd come prepared.

"If you recall, I did mention dinner today," he reminded her.

"And if *you* recall, *I* mentioned the word *no*," she countered with a defiant note.

Chris shrugged, unfazed. He dragged over a chair from another workstation.

"I just figured that was before you got hungry." He noticed that she still wasn't making a move to open any of the containers. "It's here. You might as well have some," he coaxed, opening a container close to him. She still made no move toward the food. "Were you always this stubborn?" he asked. "Or is it just me who sets you off?"

Suzie sighed. She supposed he was right. The food was here and it wasn't as if she was making some sort of a commitment if she actually ate some of it.

Erasing the unfriendly expression from her face, she peeled back the paper wrapping from a set of chopsticks, separated the two pieces and deftly clasped them in her fingers. "Thank you," she murmured almost grudgingly.

Glancing up at her, Chris stopped eating for a moment, saying, "I'm impressed."

Despite her best efforts, Suzie could feel her back going up. "Because I thanked you?" she asked, ready to tell him to take his butt off the stool and make himself scarce.

"No," he replied easily, defusing her instant reaction, "because you can use chopsticks. I'm not any good at it."

She would be the last to flatter him—nor did he need to have his ego bolstered—but what he was saying was absurd.

"It's not like playing a cello," she told him. "You just take the two pieces like so..." She demonstrated. "Then you pick up the food and bring it to your mouth, like so." She proceeded to go through the motions, slowly and elaborately.

When she was finished, Chris attempted to mimic

her actions. But he wound up failing miserably, actually sending one chopstick flying.

Unable to help herself, Suzie started to laugh at what was at best a very sad display of artlessness and ineptitude.

Rather than take offense, he appeared pleased. “So you actually *can* laugh,” he observed.

She had to say it. “At particularly hapless displays of ineptitude? Yes,” she allowed. “I can.”

“Well,” he said philosophically, “I’m always happy to please a lovely lady.”

The laughter faded and Suzie became serious again. “Don’t do that,” she told him.

“Don’t do what? Call you lovely?” Chris asked innocently.

That went without saying. She didn’t like hearing empty words of flattery, but she knew it was also pointless to tell him that. He wouldn’t listen.

“No, don’t keep trying to hit on me.” Suzie paused to consider her words. He wasn’t going to listen to that, either. “Although I guess that’s kind of like telling you not to breathe.”

Chris just smiled warmly at her. Was he humoring her or agreeing with her? She couldn’t tell.

“We can consider the possibilities while we eat,” he told her, the same warm, inviting smile on his lips.

Suzie shook her head in disbelief. She had to laugh again. When he looked at her, an unspoken question in his eyes, she explained, “You’re like that blow-up clown doll, aren’t you? The one that no matter how many times you punch it just bounces back up again—right in your face."

"Well, that's a new one," he said, rolling the image over in his mind. "Never been compared to a blow-up clown doll before."

Suzie had no idea why, but she suddenly felt bad. O'Bannon had, after all, brought her dinner even after she'd been less than friendly toward him, all but telling him to get lost.

She relented. "That wasn't exactly meant as an insult," she murmured.

And then there was the grin again, the one that belonged to the happy-go-lucky, lighthearted boy he had to have been. The one, for all she knew, he *still* was.

"I know," he told her with a conspiratorial wink.

That pulled her up short. Either they were on some kind of a wavelength she was totally unaware of, or he had one hell of an ego.

"You *know*?"

"Why don't we stop dancing around like this, Suzie Q, and eat before it gets cold?" he suggested, pulling a carton closer to him. He opened it up. "Although I have to admit I do like Chinese food cold." He raised his eyes to hers, creating, just like that, an intimate air. "For breakfast the next day."

Suzie pressed her lips together in annoyance, waiting for some sort of innuendo or maybe even a graphic scenario to follow. But there was none. There was just Chris, grappling with his chopsticks as he tried to bring at least a few strands of lo mein to his mouth.

He failed, but tried again. And again, valiantly trying to conquer the two slender pieces of polished wood and make them do his bidding.

Unable to stand it any longer, Suzie put down her own chopsticks, then picked up his and carefully positioned them in his hand.

When the result was less than successful, she tried another approach.

This time, she placed the chopsticks in his fingers and wrapped her hand around his, carefully guiding it to the contents in the container.

After three attempts, Chris, with her help, managed to secure a single morsel of shrimp. When, with her hand still around his, he brought the piece to his lips, Suzie experienced a feeling of triumph that somehow, in the next moment, seemed to transform into a completely different emotion.

She felt a warmth traveling through her limbs and torso, and even felt, heaven help her, a momentary shortness of breath that had nothing to do any condition that might have sent her hurrying to the ER, and everything to do with the man she was attempting to instruct.

Suzie pulled her hand away as if she had just come in contact with a hot frying pan filled with boiling oil.

"I think you have the hang of it," she said crisply, doing what she could to distance herself from the moment—and from the man.

"Oh, I don't know," Chris confessed. "But it certainly isn't for lack of you trying. You know," he told her with a laugh, "I think I might have discovered a brand-new kind of diet. We could call it the chopstick diet. Dexterity-challenged people like me eat all their meals using chopsticks. The pounds'll start dropping off from day one," he enthused. "And people won't have to invest in some big initial layout of cash. All they have to buy is a pair of chopsticks and then try to eat what they normally eat." He smiled broadly at her. "I can smell the success from here."

Suzie shook her head. He was actually laughing at himself. He really was one of a kind, she thought. She pushed the plastic fork toward him.

"Eat," she told him. "You don't need to lose any weight. You're fine the way you are."

Chris put his hand over his chest, feigning surprise. "Why, Suzie Q, is that a compliment?"

"That," she informed him, "was a slip of the tongue. Now eat," she ordered. "These containers can't stay here while I do my work, so once I finish eating, they're going to have to be cleared away."

"Fair enough," he agreed, nodding. "I consider myself warned."

As she watched, he picked up the chopsticks again. "Use the fork," she told him.

If he continued to eat using the chopsticks, he would be here half the night, and despite what she'd just said, she couldn't very well toss him out, not after he'd sprung for dinner the way he had—never mind that she hadn't asked him to.

But he'd already begun to eat again.

To her surprise, as she watched, Chris didn't drop anything. As a matter of fact, he was wielding the chopsticks like someone who didn't just use them on occasion, but who was very skilled with them.

When he looked up to see her watching him, her lips slightly parted in surprise, Chris set down his chopsticks for a moment.

"What can I say?" he asked with an expression she was forced—unwillingly—to describe as modest. "I learned from the very best, and you, Suzie Q, are a very skillful teacher," he concluded, adding a postscript. "Thanks for taking the time to teach me."

He was good, she thought. Ordinarily, she would have said he was a con artist. But in this case, she didn't know if O'Bannon was being genuine, or if she'd just been played.

He *did* look sincere.

Because she couldn't decide one way or the other, for now she decided to concentrate strictly on the meal, which she had to admit, with its variety, was excellent. If nothing else, Christian Cavanaugh O'Bannon did have one redeeming quality.

The detective knew where to find a good Chinese restaurant.

Chapter 5

Since he felt his best approach to a conversation was to talk to her about work, he casually asked, "Did you recognize anyone on those videos?"

Suzie shook her head. "No." She got the impression from the way he watched her that *he* had recognized someone in them. "I don't get out much," she said, reaching for an egg roll.

He'd had the same thought about the egg roll at the same time, and his fingers brushed against hers. He pulled his hand back, allowing her first choice.

"You were out last night," he reminded her, taking the second egg roll out of the container.

She'd gone to the party trying to reconnect with the person she once was. "That was a mistake," she replied decisively.

"Why?" Chris asked, studying her. "Because you met me?"

That would have made him think he mattered to her, and he didn't. Once upon a time, she would have easily been won over by his charm. But that was back when she didn't hold everything and everyone suspect. Her trust, when she actually did give it, was hard-won. So far, only Sean Cavanaugh merited it.

She gave Chris a simplistic answer. "No, because parties aren't my element anymore."

He immediately read between the lines. "But they were once."

She had no idea why it even mattered what O'Bannon thought, but she did have to work with him, at least for the time being. So she set him as straight as she could, given her circumstances. "Well, I didn't exactly grow up in a cave."

Chris easily slid to the logical question. "Where did you grow up?" he asked.

"Not here," she informed him, hoping that was the end of it.

"I kind of already picked up on that," he admitted.

Warning flags instantly went up. These days, because of her past, suspicion was never far away.

"Oh?"

Chris could sense her tension and continued talking casually. It was the only way he knew how to disarm her wariness. In some ways, she reminded him of a wild animal that had been mistreated at some point. They had to be won over with great care and patience, but once done, they turned out to be the most loyal.

He couldn't help wondering just what had happened to the woman to make her this leery.

"I asked Sean how long you'd been working here, and when he said nine months, I asked where you'd transferred from. I thought he was going to tell me the name of some other department, but he said Arizona." He smiled at her. "See, all perfectly innocent."

"Except for the part where you were asking questions about me," she pointed out.

If she meant it as an accusation, it went right by him, unnoticed. "I'm a red-blooded, single male in the prime of my life, and you're a knockout. Why wouldn't I ask questions about you?"

A knockout?

For just the slightest instance, he caught her off guard. But then she reminded herself that the man on the other end of the chopsticks was a smooth operator. She had to remember that.

"Well, for one thing, you should be asking questions about the dead woman."

"I can do both." He took another helping of the shrimp in lobster sauce. "I learned to multitask at a very early age. My mother insisted on it."

He really didn't strike her as the kind of man who listened to his mother. Or made references to her. "Your mother?"

He nodded. There was no mistaking the pride that entered his voice when he talked about the woman.

"She was widowed young, had seven kids to raise while holding down a job at the firehouse."

"She was a firefighter?" Suzie questioned incredulously.

"No. Actually, she drove an ambulance," he corrected. "We all learned to do our part and take care of one another while she was on call. On rare occasions, whenever she was too tired to move, we got to take care of her, too."

Suzie stared at him. Was he pulling her leg? He sounded sincere, but she was beginning to suspect that was just part of his con. They didn't make families like the one he claimed to have grown up in outside of old TV series.

"Aren't you laying it on rather thick?" she challenged.

Looking back, he did remember some things in a better light than they'd happened in. But that was just because of the way he felt about his family. He said as much out loud. "Maybe, but that doesn't mean it isn't true."

"Which part?" she asked, still highly skeptical. "The seven kids, the widowed mother, the ambulance job?"

"All of it," he told her simply. He could see the suspicion in her eyes again. "Hey, you want verification, you can ask your boss. Uncle Sean'll back me up."

Would he say that if it wasn't true? He should know that she would ask his uncle, and Sean Cavanaugh wasn't the kind of man to lie, even for a member of his family. "You're serious?"

"One of my very few moments, but yes. By the way," Chris said as he began to clear away the empty containers, depositing them in the paper bag he'd brought them in, "I wouldn't give up on reentering the social scene if I were you." He thought of the way his breath had backed up in his lungs when he'd first caught a glimpse of her at the party. "It wouldn't take much to get into the swing of things again."

Suzie frowned. Going out last night had been a momentary lapse in judgment on her part. She'd allowed a friend—more of an acquaintance, actually—to talk her into going with her to a club in the next city. The place was just off the coast and had sounded interesting. In a moment of weakness—and longing for the life she'd lost, a life filled with friends and good times—she'd agreed to accompany the other woman to the club. There'd been a party in progress, it turned out.

But her friend Sheila had paired off with someone less than an hour into the evening, leaving Suzie on her own. She'd been about to call a cab to take her home when her path had crossed O'Bannon's. At the time she knew him only by his sexy wink, which he'd aimed right at her the second he saw her. She had no idea that they both worked for the Aurora police department.

As soon as he started talking, she knew she was in over her head, and the first second he had turned away, she made her escape.

She hadn't exactly felt good about vanishing without a word, but it was better to be rude than to wake up with a bucketful of regrets. And the police detective with the killer smile and the sexy wink was just too sinfully good-looking to resist. She didn't need that sort of complication at this point in her life, not while she was still trying to come to terms with everything.

So, the first opportunity that came up, she'd split. "It would be harder than you might think," she told him dismissively.

But he wasn't about to be put off. "You're being way too tough on yourself, Suzie Q."

She might as well nip this in the bud now. She had no idea who'd told him that was her nickname, but she intended to set him straight.

"That's another thing. Please don't call me that. Only my friends can call me Suzie Q."

That didn't put him off. "I intend to be your friend, Suzie."

She didn't think she'd *ever* encountered anyone as brazen as this man. "What you intend and what actually happens can be two very different things," she informed him coldly.

He only smiled and said, "We'll see." Having cleared her work area of the various cartons and eating utensils he'd brought, Chris rose. "Okay, I guess can leave you to that midnight oil you wanted to burn, knowing that you won't keel over from hunger now. By the way, you might want to take a close look at the first video," he said almost too casually.

"If you look really hard, you might find that you're in for a surprise."

Suzie spent less than half a second arguing with herself over the issue. She didn't want to ask O'Bannon for details, because she thought it was all just a ploy on his part to stay longer. But in the end—a very quick end—her curiosity got the better of her. She'd watched the videos and had all but gone cross-eyed. It was obvious that she had to have missed something.

"Who is it?" she asked. When he didn't answer, she pressed, "Who did you see?"

"Why, Suzie Q, do you want me to do your work for you? Hey, that rhymes," he realized with a laugh, followed by the killer smile he seemed to be completely unaware of flashing at her.

Suzie clenched her hands before her. "Here he lies dead, after taking a blow to the head. That rhymes, too," she snapped. "Now, if you don't want that on your tombstone..."

Chris laughed. "All right, you twisted my arm. I was going to tell you anyway," he added in a whisper. "It's pretty quick, so you have to watch for it, but one of the partygoers looks like Warren Eldridge. Another one is a dead ringer for Simon Silas."

She looked at the detective uncertainly. The names were familiar, although she had no idea what either man looked like.

"The philanthropists?" she asked in disbelief.

An expression of triumphant satisfaction came

over Chris's face. "So you do get out more than you said."

That had nothing to do with it. "I read the newspaper," she corrected.

Most people he knew got their news online and couldn't be bothered with the printed page. "Newspapers, huh? My mother'd love you," he told her, throwing the takeout bag into the closest wastepaper basket.

He'd lost her again—and she was getting the impression that he enjoyed doing that.

"Why?"

"Because she thinks it's a shame that newspapers are a disappearing art form," he answered. "She says that she can remember *her* father reading the Sunday comics to her and her brothers when she was a kid."

Chris was distracting her again, Suzie thought. Tossing her a piece of useful information and then quickly burying it beneath a pile of rhetoric that had absolutely nothing to do with the case—and the case was all she cared about.

The case was *always* all she cared about, Suzie reminded herself. Because if she had been more vigilant, more alert, more into her surroundings and less into the trappings of her life, she would have realized a great deal sooner that the father she adored and worshipped—the man who made such a point of donating his time, money and effort to their local church group, to the homeless shelter; the man everyone thought so highly of—was a monster.

If she hadn't been so blinded, she would have been

able to pull back the curtain and save some of those poor girls he'd killed.

But she hadn't. And she didn't care what anyone said, that was on her.

"Hey, you okay?" Chris asked, touching her arm in an effort to get through to her.

Startled, Suzie blinked. "What? Yes, why?" She bit off the words in staccato fashion, embarrassed that she'd allowed herself to drift off like that, regressing to an earlier time, before everything fell apart.

He drew his hand away and dropped it to his side. "For a minute there you kind of turned pale on me. I thought that maybe there was something in the food you were allergic to."

"No, the only allergy I have is to people who ask a lot of invasive questions." She looked at him pointedly.

"Yeah, I know. Don't you hate that?" he asked sympathetically, as if he didn't realize she meant him. "Get some rest, Suzie Q," he advised as he began to leave. "Our victim is going to be just as dead tomorrow as she is today. Calling it a night isn't going to make any difference to her."

"But it might make a difference to the next victim," Suzie said, thinking of all the women who had been lured to their deaths because they had the same failing she had: they couldn't see beneath the surface.

That stopped him in his tracks. Chris turned around and looked at her, debating if she was just talking or if there was something in those videos he'd missed.

Or if, possibly, she knew something he didn't.

"What next victim?" he asked, the playfulness in his voice totally gone.

Suzie shrugged, silently upbraiding herself for her slip. Usually, she was a great deal more close-mouthed. What was it about this detective that made her forget to keep her guard up?

"Just a hunch," she said, hoping that would be enough for him.

She should have known better.

"Based on what?" he asked.

Based on my father. "A hunch is just a hunch, a gut feeling," she stressed impatiently, knowing she wasn't getting anywhere. She waved a dismissive hand at him. "Forget I said anything."

But Chris showed no such inclination. Instead, he was suddenly very alert and gave every indication of being on the job.

"Did I miss something?" he asked.

"Probably a lot of things," Suzie answered flippantly. But because he kept on looking at her, waiting and not saying anything, she finally told him what had just now occurred to her. "Unless someone had it in for this girl—and if they did, why not dispose of her body so no one could find it? Why deliberately leave her to be found with the leftover trash from the party?" she asked.

There was more to this, he thought. She was building toward something. "Go on," he urged.

She hadn't expected O'Bannon to listen to her to this extent. She'd thought he'd interrupt, throwing in his own, probably more elaborate, theories, not hear her out.

Because he was urging her on, she was forced to complete her thought for him. He didn't look like he was going to allow her to walk away.

"If this *wasn't* planned, then it's just a random act. And if it's a random act, maybe whoever killed this woman killed for the sheer thrill of it..." She tried not to shiver, not to dwell on that possibility at all. It was the only way she could continue to work.

"Which means he'll kill again—is that what you're saying?"

"It's plausible," she allowed, then added what she had so painfully learned. "There are more serial killers around than people might think."

Chris watched her thoughtfully. But the next moment, his more flippant side surfaced again. "I see that you're up on this month's latest 'crimes r us' magazine articles."

She was not about to get any more specific than she already had.

"Just something I picked up along the way." And that was all she was willing to say about the matter.

"Well, just in case this is actually a targeted killing and not a random-thrill one, first thing in the morning I'm going to see if any of Bethany Miller's friends can tell me if she had a jealous boyfriend, or if there was a garden-variety stalker in her life, following her around."

Where had that come from? "Bethany Miller?" Suzie questioned.

"Yeah. Oh, didn't I tell you?" he asked a bit too innocently, which meant that he damn well knew he had omitted this little bit of information he was about to unfurl. "Uncle Sean ran our victim's fingerprints through the system and got a name."

Anger smoldered in her eyes. "No, you forgot to tell me that little detail."

"I guess the prospect of breaking bread with you—or sharing chopsticks," he amended with a grin, "knocked everything else of importance right out of my head."

Yeah, right, she thought. "And is it back in now?" she asked, annoyed.

Chris's face was the essence of sheer simplicity. "Yes."

"How did you find out her name?" Suzie asked.

"Seems our victim was arrested for a DUI a year ago. Apparently, she liked to party even then." Chris saw the frown on Suzie's lips. Thinking something had occurred to her about the case, based on what he'd just told her, he asked, "What?"

She could only glare at him. "You could have told me," she said accusingly.

"Then you wouldn't have eaten with me," he pointed out cheerfully. "As it was, I found out just as I was making my run to the restaurant. Like I said, she wasn't going to get any more dead if you took a break from the case."

"Maybe I don't need to take a break from the

case," Suzie told him. "Maybe what I need is to work the case—did that ever occur to you?"

"No, but it's beginning to," he told her honestly.

She was one of those workaholics, he thought. The type that always needed to be doing something in order not to be alone with her thoughts. Why were her thoughts so bad? he wondered. Was there something in her background or her life that tormented her?

"Okay," he announced, secretly hoping he could get her to call it a day, too. "I'm going to be going now."

Instead, she merely looked at him and murmured, "Be still my heart."

She wasn't prepared for a reappearance of his kneecap-melting smile.

"Someday, Suzie Q, I'm going to get you to say that for a completely different reason," he promised quietly.

Then, before she could say something that might spoil the evening they'd just shared, he said, "I'll see you in the morning, Suzie Q, and don't worry, we'll get her killer and make the world a safer place for partying blondes."

He was looking directly at her as he said it.

And then he left before she could tell him where to go.

Chapter 6

"Hey, O'Bannon," Harold Silverberg, one of the senior detectives in the squad room, called out to Chris. It was barely eight-thirty the following morning and more than half the personnel had yet to arrive. "You've got company."

Busy looking up the address of the young woman who had, until roughly a month ago, been his victim's roommate, Chris didn't glance up at first in response to the detective's alert. By the time he did, he found himself gazing at the woman he'd shared Chinese food with last night.

Surprised and pleased, Chris smiled. She was the last person he'd expected to see in his squad room.

"Ah, so the mountain can come to Mo—"

"Save it," Suzie said, cutting him off. "I want to go with you."

Chris never skipped a beat. "Should I be pinching myself?" he asked her. "Because this sounds suspiciously like the fantasy I was having early this morning just before my alarm went off."

She should have known he'd take it the wrong way. "Not *with you*," Suzie emphasized impatiently. "I mean with you when you go interview those two philanthropists that you pointed out. Eldridge and—and..." She tried to remember the name of the second man and was coming up blank.

"Silas," Chris prompted helpfully.

The second she heard the name, she remembered. "Right, Silas," Suzie repeated. "I want to go with you when you talk to them."

"Okay," he agreed, although he had no idea why tagging along to talk to the two financial giants and well-known philanthropists would set off her eager meter. Suzie didn't strike him as a groupie and he couldn't see another reason for her wanting to be present while he interviewed either mogul. "But that's not on the agenda yet. I want to talk to Bethany's former roommate first, then ask around at the modeling agency where she worked, see if anyone can shed some light on anyone who might have wanted to hurt her."

Suzie saw no problem. "Can't you do it all?" she asked.

"Well, yes," Chris answered, "but contrary to popular opinion, not all at once." Growing serious, he added, "My partner's out on medical leave and everyone else is tied up with cases of their own, so until I can get some temporary help, it's just me working the case and there are only so many hours in the day."

Reluctantly, Suzie took the only step she could. She volunteered. That was where this was ultimately headed, anyway, she thought. "I'll help."

For once, Chris was caught completely off guard. "Excuse me?"

"You heard me," she told him, trying not to sound irritated or impatient. It wasn't exactly the best first step for this temporary partnership. "I said I'd help. I can clear it with my superior—just for this case," she qualified.

"Am I missing something here?" Chris asked. He couldn't get himself to believe that she was actually volunteering to work the case with him. He certainly liked the idea, but he'd thought she was entirely against it. "Last night, you acted as if you never wanted to see me again."

She had no desire to rehash things. She wanted to move forward. "This isn't about you, it's about the case. About Bethany Miller and whatever other victims are out there."

Something in her voice caught his attention. "Sit down," Chris prompted, indicating the chair next to his desk.

She didn't want to sit; she wanted to get started. "We don't have time to waste," she told him, a sense of urgency raising her adrenaline. The more she thought about the case, the worse it seemed to grow. They had to find Bethany's killer and stop him—or her—before someone else was killed.

But Chris wasn't going anywhere until he got a few things straight.

"Sit down," he said again, more forcefully this time.

Suzie had no choice but to do as he said. She had a feeling that O'Bannon might adopt an easy-going, laid-back air, but like the rest of his family, he couldn't be pushed anywhere he didn't want to go.

"Okay, I'm sitting," she told him, spreading her hands wide to show that she was acquiescing. "What is it that you can't say to me if I'm standing up?"

"I just didn't want to draw any undue attention to us—or you—since I got the feeling that you don't particularly like attention being turned in your direction." He watched her shift in the chair, looking somewhat uncomfortable. It just proved his theory. "Why are you suddenly so willing and eager to become my sidekick?"

"I'm *not* willing and eager—and I'm not your sidekick," she said, emphasizing her point. "But you're the lead on this case and I've just got this feeling about it..."

"What kind of feeling?" he asked.

O'Bannon was probably going to make fun of her, she thought, growing annoyed at the very idea. But she had to get him to see things her way. She wasn't just going to float along, following quietly behind him. That wasn't why she wanted to be included.

"That maybe we've just hit the tip of the iceberg," Suzie answered.

Chris had no idea where she was going with this. "Meaning?"

She wished he'd just go along with her without making her explain everything. Deep down, she knew she was right. But she hated having to convince him of it.

"Meaning there might be a lot more bodies out there that we haven't found yet." She braced herself for ridicule.

But he didn't ridicule her. Instead, he treated her hunch seriously. "What makes you think we've stumbled across a serial killer?" he asked.

Suzie blew out a breath. "Nothing I can explain yet," she was forced to admit. She felt that he'd laugh at her if she fell back on the gut-feeling explanation, and she was *not* going to tell him about her father. The problem was that the feeling she was experiencing was the same one as when she'd realized her father was the man who had killed dozens of girls over the years, girls he was supposed to have been helping. Girls who, it turned out, he'd felt sure no one would report missing because they had no one to miss them.

Braced for rejection, or worse, Suzie was surprised when she heard neither from O'Bannon. So surprised that she had to ask, "What, you're not going to laugh at me?"

His eyes looked directly into hers, as if he was

somehow communicating with her on a completely different level.

"There's nothing funny about a serial killer, and if you believe we're dealing with one, well, Suzie Q, I guess that's good enough for me," he told her.

She eyed him uncertainly, waiting for a punch line. He had to be up to something. It couldn't be this easy.

"Just like that?" she questioned. "You're going along with me because I have a hunch?"

Chris got the impression that he believed in her more than Suzie believed in herself. That had to be hard for her. And yet she was here, making her pitch, so she had to believe this more than she consciously realized.

"Uncle Sean made it clear that he believes in you, and I believe in him. So, like my old math teacher worked so hard to drum into my head, if A equals B and B equals C, then A equals C."

"Algebra," she corrected quietly.

He wasn't sure if he'd heard her right. "What?"

"You said math, but it's algebra," she told him. "You're quoting an algebra axiom."

Rather than get annoyed, he laughed. "See? Having you around is making me smarter already." But he needed to find out something before he got in too deeply with this. "Just tell me one thing. Is there any particular reason *why* you think that Eldridge and Silas have something to do with Bethany's murder?"

"I didn't mean to make is sound as if they were working in concert on this."

"So you're leaning toward a solo performance," he said, building on the terminology she'd just used. "Okay, the question's still the same. What's the reason? Something has to have set you off and pointed you in that general direction. So what was it?" Chris asked.

Suzie pressed her lips together. "I magnified the scene that they're in."

He didn't understand, but he gave her a chance to elaborate. "I'm listening."

Because he was, Suzie began to lose some of her nerve. Maybe her reasoning was faulty. Maybe she was wrong. And maybe she was allowing what had happened in her own life to color what she thought she was seeing now. She needed to go over this again for her own peace of mind before cluing him in.

"Never mind."

"Look, you came all this way, you even did an about-face on working with me, so something had to have gotten to you. All I did was ask you one simple question. You should be able to share your thinking on this if you expect to eventually go to a judge with probable cause."

Her mind was scrambling and he'd lost her for a second. "What?"

Chris explained it to her patiently. "If there's anything to this theory you're not sharing with me, now's the time to let me know. Somewhere along the line we're going to need search warrants to look for telltale evidence. In order to get that, we need probable cause to light a fire under the judge. You said you had a gut feeling, but gut feelings are based on intuition. You've got to give me something to work with here."

Suzie took baby steps. "It was his expression," she told O'Bannon, thinking of Eldridge.

"You picked up on an expression on that grainy cut?" Chris asked, impressed.

She doled out each word as if it was precious and scarce. "I enhanced it."

"You're a computer geek?" he asked, surprised. "Sorry, I mean you're a computer tech?" She hadn't mentioned this to him before.

"No," she admitted. When he continued to look at her, waiting for an explanation, she finally told him, "But I know how to work my way through YouTube. You can find a tutorial there on almost anything. I found one on how to enhance a piece of video footage."

He hadn't expected that. "Okay, we'll talk more about your enhancement prowess in a minute. Right now, tell me more about this expression that has you so fired up."

With each word she uttered, a shiver went down her spine, because the situation just reminded her of what she'd experienced looking at her father once the truth had come out.

Hindsight, she'd come to discover, could be extremely painful.

"It was smug, like he was about to get something he wanted—something he *really* wanted."

Chris interpreted what was behind the expression in a slightly different light. "Eldridge can buy and sell half of the state. The man's on the board of over twenty different corporations and foundations. There's no doubt in my mind that he was going to get whatever he wanted to get."

She shook her head. O'Bannon didn't understand—how could he? No one in his family was a monster. He didn't know what it was like to unwittingly live with someone like that, to look back and reevaluate every moment he'd lived through.

"It was more intense than that," she insisted. "It almost didn't look…" She paused for a moment, hesitating to use the word. And then she finally gave in. There was no other word she could substitute. "Human. It almost didn't look human," she repeated.

Chris studied her for a long moment before he spoke. "You make it sound like you recognized that look. Like you've seen it before."

Again, she debated the wisdom of telling him this, but if she didn't, if she just backed away, how would she feel if it turned out that she was right—and another girl died because she didn't want to open up a box that for personal reasons she felt was best left closed?

"I have."

He found that hard to believe. Suzie struck him as rather young, and according to her own admission, she hadn't been part of the CSI division in Aurora for more than nine months.

"Where?" he challenged.

She was *not* about to go into that. Not about to pull off the scab beneath the Band-Aid that was barely hanging on. Instead, she took refuge in vague terms. "I deal with a lot of criminals."

"You deal with the evidence left by a lot of criminals," he corrected. "That doesn't give you firsthand knowledge or face-to-face dealings with killers, let alone with serial killers," Chris pointed out.

She used his own words as a jumping-off point. "Which I'll get if you let me come with you," she insisted. "You just said yourself that you're down a man. I can fill that spot."

It was the word *man* that struck him. His gaze washed over her, a hint of a smile playing on his lips. "Not hardly."

"The spot of an investigator," she told him pointedly, knowing exactly what he was thinking. "Look, it's not unheard of for a detective to work with a crime scene investigator. It's done all the time." She paused. When he didn't immediately agree, she told him, "If you don't want me to come with you, fine, I can do some investigating on my own."

He could see her getting into trouble. See it vividly. And it would be on his head even if no one else pointed a finger at him. He didn't want her getting hurt, and she seemed so determined to avenge the dead woman, she would blindly charge in where proverbial angels feared to go.

Like it or not, he needed to team up with her for the duration of this.

"Simmer down, Masked Avenger, you can come with me," he told Suzie, relenting because he had no other choice and he knew it. “But make no mistake, we’re going to play by my rules.”

“Fair enough,” she allowed, although silently, she couldn’t help wondering just what she was letting herself in for.

She wasn’t happy about this alliance. And if it wasn’t for the fact that some unknown force seemed to be urging her on, telling her that if she hung back on the sidelines, the next dead girl would be on her, she would have told O’Bannon just what he could do with his rules and where he could put them.

“That means before we go and try to rope ourselves a couple of billionaires who are on the board of practically every nonprofit foundation and organization in the state, we go and talk to Bethany’s former roommate,” he told Suzie.

“And ask her what?” she inquired, thinking that every minute they pursued this line of questioning was a minute more that the killer could be snuffing out another life, or at least making plans to do that.

She couldn’t have forgotten what they’d talked about last night. “Remember those theories about a possible jealous boyfriend or a stalker we spoke about over fried rice? Well, her ex-roommate might be the one who could tell us about that. She might also know if Bethany was seeing some over-the-top rich guy she couldn’t talk about.” And then, before Suzie had a chance to bring up the obvious, he beat her to it. “And in my experience, roommates *always* talk about the rich guy their roommates can’t talk about.”

Suzie frowned, wading through the detective's sea of rhetoric. Why couldn't O'Bannon be stoic, like a normal man? Why did he feel compelled to talk until she felt as if she was drowning in words? She found it really annoying.

Most of all, she found the way he seemed to get under her skin *really* annoying.

"All right, we'll do it your way," she told Chris grudgingly, resigned to the fact that she wouldn't be able to take part in the investigation the way she wanted to until she jumped through the hoops he was holding up.

"You sure that my uncle is all right with you working with me on this?" he asked.

Sean Cavanaugh was as easygoing as they came. It didn't take much interaction with him to know that, but everyone had their idiosyncrasy, the one thing that might set them off. Chris didn't want to inadvertently be a party to something that might cause waves between his uncle and Suzie. However, he was perfectly willing to talk to him about this temporary arrangement if that was necessary.

"I'm sure it will be."

"*Will* be," he repeated, immediately picking up on the future tense. He knew what that meant. "In other words, you haven't asked yet."

"I wanted to feel you out first," Susie told him honestly.

It wasn't the spirit of honesty that kept Chris from echoing the statement back at her—with possibly a substitution for the word *out*. Rather, it was the spirit of survival that kept him from making a comment about his willingness to be "felt" by her.

"Okay, you've done that. Maybe I should be the one to talk to Sean about you lending a hand in the field with this investigation."

She didn't think of Chris as being diplomatic. Neither did she think of him as the best person to convince Sean that she felt it was really necessary for her to get involved, from an investigative standpoint.

"No," she responded, "that's all right. I'll just give him a call about it from the road."

Chris looked at her uncertainly. "The road?"

She stood up, ready to go. "While you're driving. To get this interview with the ex-roommate over with," she prompted, when O'Bannon didn't immediately pick up on her meaning.

"Sounds good to me," he told her as they left the squad room.

The way he said that made Suzie wonder if perhaps she had just suggested something she was going to live to regret.

Chapter 7

The apartment that Bethany Miller had lived in until just recently was located in a fifteen-story high-rise that was barely eight years old. The building itself was in an upscale area of Aurora that was growing only more so.

Chris drove into the underground parking structure and then he and Suzie rode up to the seventh floor.

"Looks like a place to aspire to, not move out of," he commented as they got out of the elevator.

"Maybe someone told her she could do better," Suzie guessed. She felt that at twenty-four, which was how old Bethany was, the young woman could have been easily manipulated and talked into anything. It wouldn't take much.

"The roommate's name is Shelley West and she's in apartment 7D," Chris announced, looking to either side of him to check the letters. "This way," he said the next moment, turning to his left.

Apartment 7D was tucked into a corner, with a lavish painting of blue orchids hanging on the wall not far from the door.

Chris rang the doorbell and waited. Then rang again. When there was still no answer, he knocked.

"Maybe she's not home," Suzie speculated, five seconds before the door finally opened. Not all the way, just a crack.

"Sorry, whatever you're selling, I don't want any," the rather statuesque, annoyed looking blonde in the doorway said just before she began to close the door again.

The slim opening was all Chris needed. He quickly stuck his foot in to keep the woman from closing the door again.

"We're not selling anything," he informed her. "I'm Detective O'Bannon and this is CSI Quinn. We're with the Aurora Police Department and we'd like to talk to you for a few minutes."

The woman seemed to soften slightly as she took another look at Chris. It was obvious to Suzie that the blonde liked what she saw.

"Now isn't a good time, but if you come back tonight," Bethany's former roommate suggested warmly, addressing only Chris, "maybe we could talk then."

"This won't take long, Ms. West," Chris promised.

"We'd just like to ask you a few questions about your former roommate, Bethany Miller."

The smile on Shelley's face disappeared, and she became all business. "Like I said, now isn't a good time."

"She's dead," Suzie said, when it looked as if the woman was going to try to push her way past them to get to the elevator.

That brought Shelley to a dead stop. Obviously stunned, she glanced from Suzie to the detective. "What?"

Chris gave her a little more information, watching her expression as he spoke. "Someone killed her Sunday night," he stated.

A small gasp of horror escaped her lips and she immediately cried, "Was it Justin?" She looked from one of them to the other. "Did that bastard kill her?" she demanded.

They had a possible suspect, Chris thought, pleased.

"Why don't we step inside your apartment and talk about it?"

He took the woman's elbow and guided her back into her apartment, since she appeared to be momentarily unaware of her surroundings or what she was doing.

"Did she suffer?" Shelley asked him, concerned. "Bethany, did she suffer?"

"No," Suzie answered quickly and decisively, before Chris had a chance to say anything. The roommate might have seemed unwilling to talk about

Bethany to begin with, but the news of her murder obviously changed the situation. Suzie felt for her. "She died instantly."

Chris glared at her. They hadn't gotten the ME's report back yet, so there was no way of knowing any of the details involved in the young blonde's death. What Suzie was saying was pure conjecture. Why was she telling Shelley that?

"You mentioned a Justin," he prodded, once the stunned woman sat on the sofa. "Was that the name of Bethany's boyfriend?"

"Ex-boyfriend," she corrected. She was sitting on the edge of the cushion, as if ready to jump to her feet at any second. Shock? Or was there another reason she looked like that? Chris wondered. "She dumped him around the same time that she moved out. Said she wanted more out of life than a boyfriend who was going nowhere and a seventh floor apartment she had to share with a roommate. Bethany said she had plans. Big plans." The words sounded bitter as Shelley repeated them.

"Did Bethany share any of those plans with you?" Suzie asked her.

But the other woman shook her head. "All she said was that her life was about to explode."

"Apparently," Suzie murmured under her breath. Chris shot her a warning look, but Bethany's former roommate didn't appear to have heard.

"How did Justin feel about all this?" Chris asked.

"How do you think he felt?" Shelley cried. "He was angry. I heard them arguing about it just before she moved out. He was yelling that he wasn't going to give up until he talked some sense into her."

"Maybe his definition of 'sense' is different than ours," Suzie speculated. "Do you know this Justin's last name?"

Shelley paused for a minute, clearly thinking. "Sellers," she told them. "That's it. Justin Sellers."

Suzie saw the detective inputting something into his phone. She assumed it was the boyfriend's last name. "Would you happen to know where he lives?"

Shelley shook her head. "Bethany never mentioned it. Just that it wasn't up to her standards. But I know he got a job as a barista at one of those coffee shops in the new mall. You know, the one they opened up across from the Main Place movie theaters."

"How did she die?" she asked, almost timidly in comparison to the anger she'd displayed when she'd opened the door. "Bethany was always afraid of drowning, because she couldn't swim." She looked from the detective to the woman with him. "She wasn't drowned, was she?"

"She was strangled," Chris answered, watching the young woman's face closely.

Shelley shivered. "Just like Rosemary," she whispered.

It was Suzie who was instantly alert. "Who's Rosemary?" she asked.

"My last roommate." The words were no sooner out of Shelley's mouth than her eyes flew open in horror as she absorbed what she'd just said. "Oh my

God, I'm jinxed." The second she pronounced herself that, she sought to have her assumption invalidated. "You don't think I'm really jinxed, do you?"

She was almost begging one of them to tell her that she wasn't.

"You had another roommate who was strangled?" Chris asked incredulously. It seemed like a hell of a coincidence to him. Most people didn't have one roommate who was killed, let alone two, the same way.

This time, instead of remaining on the edge of her seat, Shelley collapsed back on the sofa, as if the weight of what she was thinking had gotten too heavy for her to bear.

"When I was in college. She was my roommate at the dorm, actually." Details came back to her in fragmented pieces as she spoke. "I hardly knew her, except that she loved to party. Say the word *party* and Rosemary was the first one there," Shelley recalled.

"Would you happen to have a picture of her?" Suzie asked.

She saw O'Bannon watching her, but she didn't want to take the time to explain what she was thinking. Not yet. Possibly not ever if she turned out to be wrong.

"No," Shelley answered, then thought again. "Wait. Maybe." Taking out her cell phone, she went through the pictures she had stored there. Finding what she was looking for, she held it up for them to see. "Here, this was Rosemary."

After looking at the photo, Suzie passed the phone

to the detective. By his expression, she could see that O'Bannon was thinking the same thing she was. Rosemary and Bethany could have passed for sisters.

"Did they ever find whoever killed Rosemary?" Chris asked.

Shelley shook her head. "They found Rosemary's body the morning after the big fund-raiser."

"Fund-raiser?" Suzie repeated.

"My senior year, a couple of years ago," Shelley said. "The university's donors threw this big fund-raiser right after our football team won the championship. Rosemary thought it would be the perfect time to make some connections. She said she intended to be somebody, and what better place to start than where all the money people were gathered?"

It was obvious that now that the memory had surfaced, it was painful for Shelley to deal with.

"Did you attend the fund-raiser?" Chris asked.

Shelley shook her head. "I had midterms to study for. I'm not much on partying," she confessed. "I'm beginning to think it's safer that way."

"You might be right," he agreed. "Why don't you give me all the details that you can remember about Rosemary's death—starting with her last name."

Suzie looked at the detective, surprised. So she wasn't the only one who thought there might be a connection between the two deaths. She felt vindicated—and oddly unsettled at the same time.

"Ames. Her last name was Ames," Shelley was saying. "She had this little card made up that read

Rosemary Ames to Please. I told her it sounded like a hooker's card. She got mad."

"For the record," Chris told her, "I think you were probably right."

Shelley's eyes widened. "You think that's why she wound up dead?" she asked, horrified.

"Let's just take this one step at a time," he told her.

Chris proceeded to take down the information that the young woman gave him. She couldn't remember the name of the investigating detective, but she did know that the killer was never found. It was what had prompted her to move off campus, she confided.

Nodding, Chris took more notes.

"You seemed to be listening awfully intently back there," Chris noted as they got back into his car after they left Shelley West's apartment. "Something strike you as off?"

Suzie meted out her words carefully. She'd learned not to reveal too much until she was certain of both her facts and her audience. "I was just watching Shelley's face when she was telling you about what happened to her college roommate."

"And?" He couldn't help wondering why the words had to be all but dragged out of Suzie's mouth. He wasn't used to that. He'd grown up with sisters who never hesitated saying what was on their minds—whether he wanted to hear it or not. "Do you think she killed either of her roommates?"

"No, I don't," Suzie told him. "I think she looked genuinely surprised and horrified that her roommates were strangled. I also think that she'll probably go to bed with all the lights on tonight. Maybe for the next week—if not longer," she commented, thinking of how wide the young woman's eyes were when she was relaying the details about her college roommate.

Chris nodded. "Probably. Right now I'm more interested in this boyfriend who didn't want to take no for an answer."

Suzie still couldn't shake the feeling that this was bigger than just a jealous possessive boyfriend. "That might explain Bethany's murder, but what about Rosemary's?"

Their concern was Bethany's murder. They hadn't even heard about the other one before this morning. "Could be unrelated," Chris pointed out, his expression giving nothing away.

"Could be," Suzie allowed. "But from Shelley's description, the MO is the same." And that was the sort of detail that always seemed to tie things up with a bow.

"From Shelley's description," he repeated pointedly. The young woman could have gotten her facts confused, or remembered them wrong, he thought. "Let's see if we can pull the report on that case, see if our ME thinks the same person killed both of them." He paused as he came to a stop at a red light, then glanced in her direction. "Looks like you were right."

Suzie had learned to be on her guard almost constantly, even when it came to flattery. "About?"

"We might be chasing a serial killer." She sighed

beside him. The light turned green, but he spared her another glance before putting his foot on the accelerator. "What's the matter? I thought you'd be pleased about being right."

"Pleased?" she echoed in disbelief.

He heard her voice go up at the end of the word. Chris realized he was treading on sensitive ground and he had no idea why.

"Wrong word," he told her. "Not pleased. But it has to be gratifying to be right."

"It would be more gratifying if I was wrong," she told him, staring straight ahead at the road. "The last thing the world needs is another serial killer."

"Agreed." He paused a second, trying to word this carefully, since his last statement seemed to have upset something. "Well, maybe by working together, we can end his 'spree' before the count gets too high."

"If it hasn't already," she murmured under her breath.

Chris had never been the kind to tiptoe around things and it obviously was getting him nowhere this time, either. The direct approach was called for here, he thought.

"Is there something that you're not telling me?" Chris asked. "Something you know that I don't?"

She squared her shoulders, still staring straight ahead. "Only that he has to be stopped."

"No argument there."

Suzie debated a second, then allowed just the tiniest piece of her past out, generalizing it. "And that he could be in plain sight," she added, thinking of all the times the police had gone right by their house, never once stopping to question the scout leader that everyone trusted, the dedicated dad who'd palled around with the police force and remained above suspicion for so many years. It made her want to cry every time she thought about it.

"He might be," Chris allowed. "But if this *is* a serial killer, FBI profilers say that most of them are loners who have low-level jobs and in general just don't fit in."

"Most," she repeated, knowing she should leave it at that. But she couldn't. "Most doesn't mean all, though."

There *was* something Suzie wasn't telling him, but Chris had no way of getting it out of her if she didn't want to tell him. He tried another approach. "Where did you say you worked before you came here?" Sean had told him Arizona, but maybe that was incorrect.

He noticed she shifted in her seat before answering. *Why?*

"Arizona."

All right, she was giving him the same answer she'd given Sean. But Chris wanted more. "Where in Arizona?" he pressed, keeping his tone friendly.

"Phoenix." Suzie could feel herself getting defensive. Why was he asking her these questions? "My résumé's on file," she informed him.

He merely smiled in response. "Looking you up

would be too much like snooping. I've always liked the personal touch myself."

"Well, for your sake, I hope someone touches you personally someday. Meanwhile, we've got more questions about this case than answers," she pointed out. "We should be focusing on that."

"Multitasking, remember? I can do both."

"Don't spread yourself too thin," she warned.

"Worried about me?" he asked, amused.

"Worried that if you go down, you'll take me with you."

The sexy grin on his lips told her that he wasn't interpreting her words the way she meant them. "Count on it."

Suzie decided that it was in her best interest not to respond.

The District Shopping Center was closer than the police station, so he drove there first.

The newly constructed center had its share of the usual stores and an overage of restaurants, catering to an eclectic variety of tastes. But there was only one coffee shop in the center—if they didn't count the popular doughnut chain shop that was the first thing shoppers saw when they turned in off the thoroughfare.

"He might not be on duty," Suzie pointed out.

Chris had already thought of that. "Then we'll ask the manager for his address," he answered, as they entered the coffee shop.

At least half a dozen enticing aromas greeted them

as they went in. One of the clerks behind the counter pointed out the manager, who looked as if he was barely old enough to shave.

"How can I serve Aurora's finest?" the young man asked solicitously when he was shown their credentials.

"You can tell us when Justin Sellers is coming in," Chris answered.

The moment he heard Justin's name, the manager's sunny smile disappeared. "He's not. That SOB quit in the middle of his shift."

Chris looked at him sharply. "When?"

It was obvious that it pained the man to even talk about Sellers. "A couple of weeks ago," he all but snarled. "You see him, you tell him that even if he comes crawling back on his knees across broken glass, he's not getting his job back."

"You two had words?" Chris guessed.

"Words?" The manager's voice rose an octave. "He cursed me out. Cursed out everybody in the store. That idiot would have smashed my best coffeemaker if I hadn't stopped him."

"He was going to break a machine?" Suzie questioned. It sounded as if the ex-boyfriend had gone on a rampage. Was it because of Bethany?

"No," the manager corrected impatiently. "He was going to punch Jose out. Jose's my best coffeemaker." He waved a hand, indicating a man behind the counter who looked as if he was filling several orders at once. "Moves like the wind."

"Would you have Justin's address on file?" Chris asked, trying to get them back to the main topic.

"You're in luck," he informed them, leading the way back to his tiny office. "I was going to purge it out of my files at the end of the month. It's not like I'm ever going to let the guy come back, after that stunt."

He scrolled through a file that was open on his computer. "Here," he declared, jabbing a finger at the screen. "Here's his address. I'll print it up." A moment later he handed Chris the printed sheet. "When you see him, tell him I hope he rots in hell."

Folding the paper, Chris tucked it into his suit pocket. "Thanks, I'll pass along the message."

"Oh," the manager called, when they began to leave the shop. "What's this all about, anyway?"

Chris retraced his steps, not about to shout the words across the crowded shop, and Suzie followed.

"His ex-girlfriend was murdered," he said, once they'd reached the manager again. "We'd just like to ask him a few questions."

A knowing smirk crossed the man's lips. "Sellers probably did it. Never could keep that temper of his under control."

Suzie had to ask. "If you don't mind me inquiring, with all that going against him, why would you keep him on?"

The man blew out a breath, as if admitting something pained him. "He could be really charming when he wanted to be. You should have seen all the women lining up here for their morning coffee. I've got a feeling that half of them didn't even drink coffee. They just bought it to flirt with Sellers." He shook his head. "No accounting for taste," he declared.

"None," Chris agreed. Moving quickly, he made it to the exit before the manager could say anything further. He held the door for Suzie, then followed her out. "Sellers might be our man, after all," he said.

"Might be," she agreed, but without conviction. Something told her that it couldn't really be that easy. It never was.

Besides, O'Bannon was forgetting one important little fact. If Sellers killed Bethany, then who killed Shelley's first roommate, Rosemary?

Suzie couldn't shake the feeling that the two young women looking alike was not a coincidence, but a contributing factor to the crime.

Chapter 8

Chris waited until they had gotten back into his car before saying anything regarding the interview they'd just had about the victim's ex-boyfriend.

His seat belt secured, he looked at Suzie as he put his key into the ignition. "You don't think so, do you?"

She'd just buckled up, her mind admittedly elsewhere. "What?"

He stated it more clearly. "You don't think that Sellers is our killer."

She didn't, but until she could come up with evidence to back her up, she didn't want to get into any kind of a long-winded discussion with O'Bannon over this.

"I didn't say that."

Easing out of the shopping center, he made a left turn and got back on the main drag. "You didn't have to. Your tone of voice did."

She really wished O'Bannon would stop trying to pin her down all the time. "So now you're into voice interpretation?"

He took no offense at her tone. "Hey, I'm a detective. It's what I do." Becoming serious, he urged her, "Tell me why you think it's not him."

He was still trying to pin her down. "I don't know it's not him," she protested.

Chris wasn't going to give up easily. "But…?" he asked, waiting.

Sensing that he wasn't going to back off, she gave in and told him what was bothering her about pegging Sellers as the killer. "It just seems too simple somehow."

"When you hear hoofbeats, it's usually a horse," Chris reminded her.

"And every so often," she countered, "it *does* turn out to be a zebra. I'm not saying we don't question Sellers, I'm just saying we need to keep an open mind while we're doing it."

At this early stage of the investigation, he had no problem with that. But he also wanted her input. "Tell me what your open mind is telling you."

Suzie frowned. She didn't like sharing things until she was absolutely sure of the facts and the person she was sharing them with, and in this case, she knew very little about either, especially the latter.

She shrugged, looking out the side window. "Maybe later."

He wasn't about to let her brush him off. "Maybe now, Suzie Q," he told her firmly. "I didn't bring you along for your pretty face—although that is a bonus," he allowed. "Uncle Sean thinks you could be the best crime scene investigator he's ever had. Show me why he thinks that."

Was O'Bannon just flirting with her, or did he really want to know? She wasn't sure, but she decided to share a little of what she was thinking.

"Does it make any sense that Bethany broke up with Sellers and then gets back with him just before this blowout of a bash, which definitely had to be the thing she was into? From the looks of it, all the beautiful people were there, and I got the sense that she really wanted to be part of that world. Sellers would have just cramped her style, so why bring him?"

Chris thought he had an answer for that. "Maybe she didn't bring him along. Maybe he followed her there, waited for his chance, and then when she was alone, dragged her off and gave her an ultimatum—choose him or this new lifestyle. When Bethany chose the latter, he killed her."

"You just said it yourself—she wouldn't have gone off with him willingly," Suzie insisted. "If Sellers tried to drag her off, she would've made noise, a lot of noise. No matter how loud that party was, *someone* would have heard. No, whoever killed her, I think it was someone she trusted." Suzie clenched her jaw, thinking of Bethany's last moments. "She never saw it coming."

"Sounds like your theory might have possibilities," he agreed. "But I still want to talk to Sellers."

"Best way to rule him out if it's not him," she agreed.

His uncle was right, he thought as he drove. This one really did have a lot of potential—in more ways than one.

No one answered the door when he knocked. Not even when he knocked hard the third time.

"Maybe he's out, looking for a new job," Suzie suggested.

"Or maybe he's just out," Chris told her, peering in through the kitchen window, which looked out on the courtyard. He beckoned Suzie over.

When she joined him and gazed through the glass, Suzie saw what he was referring to. There was a man sprawled out, facedown, on the kitchen floor. It was obvious that he was unconscious.

"You think he's dead, too?" she asked, reassessing her theory.

"Dead drunk is probably more like it," Chris told her. He pointed to the figure. "I don't see any signs of blood on the floor around him." Walking away from Suzy, he said, "Since he's unconscious, I'll go see if the apartment rental manager is in so he can open the guy's door for us."

"Don't bother getting the manager," Suzie called after him.

Chris turned around. "You want to come back?" he inquired.

"No, I want *you* to come back." Suzie slipped something that resembled a nail file back into her messenger bag and pointed to the apartment door, which was now standing open.

"The door wasn't locked?" Chris asked, surprised. He could have sworn he'd tried the doorknob when there'd been no answer. There had been no give when he'd turned it.

Suzie smiled as he rejoined her. "It wasn't when I finished with it."

He raised an eyebrow, waiting for more. "'Finished with it'?"

She didn't want to go into details. He'd probably think she was bragging.

"Just call it standard CSI training," she told him, gesturing for him to enter.

"Not from what I've heard," Chris replied. But it was obvious he was not about to stand on ceremony or remind her about there being rules against breaking and entering. Instead, he said, "Nice work, Suzie Q," and walked into the eight-hundred-square-foot apartment.

Chris went directly to the man lying on the floor. After satisfying himself that Sellers did have a pulse, he shook him and cheerfully announced, "Rise and shine, Sellers. Time to wake up and start talking."

"You think that he's drunk?" Suzie asked. Getting on the unconscious man's other side, she slipped her arm under his and proceeded to help Chris lift him off the floor.

"I think he drank some whole damn bar dry," Chris told her, having the misfortune of taking a deep breath as he maneuvered him up. The man fairly reeked of alcohol.

"He's heavier than he looks," Suzie grunted, as they struggled to get him upright on a kitchen chair.

"That's because every inch of him is completely filled with booze," Chris told her. He exhaled as he took a step back. "I wouldn't recommend lighting a match around this guy for the next twenty-four hours," he said, only half kidding. "Does he have any coffee?" he asked Suzie, who was already going through the cupboard, looking for the very same thing.

"Just instant," she concluded, finally finding a half-empty jar of a popular brand.

"And he calls himself a barista." Chris pretended to scoff. "Okay, boil some water and let's start getting that stuff into him."

She did as he suggested, turning on the low-end coffeemaker Sellers had on the counter.

By the time they got a third cup of coffee into him, Sellers was fairly awake and demanding to know who the hell they were and what the hell they were doing in his apartment.

Deciding that the man was sober enough, Chris stopped forcing the black liquid into him. "We're with the Aurora Police Department, and right now, we're trying to get you sober."

"Don't!" Seller ordered, pushing him back. "I'll only have to get drunk again."

After putting the mug down, Chris crossed his arms before him and studied the man. "Any particular reason?" he asked.

"That's none of your damn business," Sellers snapped angrily. Dragging a hand through his unruly hair, he started to get up. But he was unsteady on his feet and immediately sank back down in his chair.

"Where were you last night—and before you tell us it's none of our damn business," Chris warned pointedly, "it is. It's official police business and you need to be honest with us."

Sellers was scowling so hard his eyebrows all but covered his eyes. "I was at the same place I am every night," he muttered. Taking a breath, he added, "The Saint."

That didn't make any sense to her. Suzie came to the only conclusion she could, given the fragmented information. "You were in church?"

"No, The *Saint*," Sellers repeated, this time with more emphasis. Seeing that he wasn't getting through, he huffed and said, "It's a local bar. Only damn place I can get to within walking distance." He blinked several times and focused on Suzie. Seeing her for the first time, he asked, "Hey, are you with anyone?"

"I'm with the police department," she informed him stiffly.

"No, I mean with a man," Sellers said insistently, drawing himself up as if he was about to make a pitch for her.

"She's with me," Chris told him, before she could say anything that would prolong this line of questioning on Sellers's part. The man was hitting on her and they didn't have time for this. The fact that it annoyed him was something he'd revisit at another time.

"Oh." Sellers's face fell noticeably. "It figures," he muttered. "All the gorgeous ones are taken."

"Hey, Sellers, concentrate," Chris instructed, snapping his fingers to bring the man's attention back to him. "Did anyone see you at this bar?"

The man looked at him as if he was talking nonsense. "Sure, someone saw me at the bar. What do you think I am, invisible? She acts like I'm invisible," he complained, talking to his shoes as if they could hear him. "But I'm not, and someday she's going to be sorry she treated me like that."

"Who's going to be sorry?" Suzie asked, before Chris could beat her to it.

"Bethany!" he shouted. "Bethany's going to be sorry she dumped me. I'm going to *make* her sorry," he said, becoming so animated that he almost fell off his chair.

Chris managed to catch him at the last moment, steadying Sellers as he righted him, then patted the man on his shoulder.

"First things first, Sellers," he told him. "Can you

give us the names of some of the people who saw you at the bar two nights ago?"

Sellers appeared to be thinking the question over. "I could," he answered.

Chris looked around for a piece of paper and something to write with. He didn't know how long Sellers would be willing to cooperate.

Finally, Chris took out the sheet the coffee shop manager had given him with Sellers's address on it. Flipping the paper over, he handed Sellers the pen he found on the counter.

"Write them down," he instructed.

The man was blinking, obviously trying to focus on the blank paper. He started to write, then stopped. "Does neatness count?" he asked, slurring his words.

"Not this time," Chris assured him, guiding the man's hand back to the paper. "Just get the spelling right."

"Hey, man, I never asked nobody to spell their name for me," Sellers protested.

"Just do the best you can," Suzie told him.

He leered at her. "I can do better if you give me a little encouragement, honey."

"Just write," Chris ordered. "Before she's tempted to break your hand."

Muttering under his breath, Sellers wrote. He managed to get a total of three names on the paper before passing out again. As the pen slipped from his hand, the former barista slid bonelessly onto the floor.

Suzie jumped back to get out of his way. She surveyed the slumped form, shaking her head. "How can a man consume that much alcohol and still live?" she marveled.

Chris looked over the names Sellers had written, then folded the paper again and put it back into his pocket. They were barely legible, but he could make them out.

He laughed at Suzie's comment. "You should have met some of the guys in my dorm. On second thought, maybe it's better that you didn't."

"So does Sellers have his alibi?" Suzie asked.

"We'll find that out when we locate these men and talk to them."

"From what Sellers said, our best bet is to go to that bar he mentioned and ask the bartender. He should be able to tell us where to find the men Sellers named—not to mention maybe back up his story, as well."

Chris nodded. "Yeah, that should get Sellers off our suspect list."

"We're just going to leave him here?" Suzie questioned. O'Bannon had been rather keen on the man being the killer just a little while ago, but now he wasn't taking him in. She didn't understand. Had she missed something?

The detective stopped at the door. "Well, he's got no job, and I'm pretty sure if he wakes up, he's just going to reacquaint himself with the contents of that bottle he has over there." He pointed it out. "So my guess is that, at least for the time being, Sellers is not about to go anywhere."

"But we are," she assumed, judging by Chris's body language.

He nodded. "You're pretty good at this," he said. In all honesty, he'd had no idea what to expect when he'd taken her on today, and he had to admit that he was pleased it was working out. "We're going to Autopsy."

"Did you get a call?" she asked, as she got back into his car.

"No, not yet, but I think the medical examiner has to be finished with the preliminary report by now. They should know time of death, as well as if they found any skin or fibers under the victim's nails. I want to find out if there's any indication that she fought for her life."

Suzie sighed, thinking of the victims her father had lulled into a false sense of security before he'd snuffed out their lives. "She might not have realized that she had to," Suzie said under her breath.

Making a right turn, he glanced at her quizzically. "Did you say something?"

She shook her head. "Nothing important."

But she had said something, he was sure. "Why don't you let me be the judge of that?" he coaxed. "Sometimes it's the throwaway lines that lead to solving a case."

Suzie frowned. She was about to tell him that it really was nothing, but then thought better of it and shrugged. "I said that she might not have known that she had to fight for her life." Suzie enunciated each word so she wouldn't have to repeat them again.

"You mean because whoever strangled her was someone she trusted."

"Or someone who she really wanted to trust," Suzie added.

"That's pretty insightful," Chris mused.

"Not really." Insight had nothing to do with it. Living through the horrible weeks of her father's trial was what had made her think of it.

"If Sellers's alibi holds up," Chris was saying as he pulled into the police parking lot, "we're going with that," he acknowledged, referring to what she had just said.

He expected her to look pleased. Instead, she almost looked sad. What was up with that?

Chapter 9

There was only one live occupant in the medical examiner's room when he and Suzie walked in, and it was not the person Chris was looking for.

"Hi, is Kristin around?" he asked the dour man bent over the notes he was inputting on the computer.

The latter was located on the ME's undersized, scarred desk, which in turn sat against the wall, out of the way of general foot traffic.

Dr. Martin Rowe looked at them over the top of his rimless glasses. In his late fifties, with thinning hair that was on its way to being nonexistent in several patches, the ME appeared less than pleased that the police detective invading his space was asking for the whereabouts of a junior colleague.

"She got called away on family business. You

would know more about that than I would," Rowe told him, pursing his thin lips.

"Kristin" was Dr. Kristin Alberghetti, the newest "almost Cavanaugh" to have joined the ever-expanding ranks. Engaged to his cousin Malloy, she would be the first doctor in the family once the wedding took place, as his mother had pointed out.

More than once, as he recalled.

Chris kept his voice light and friendly. "Just thought she might be here." And she, he had a feeling, would be a lot easier to get information out of than Dr. Rowe, who looked as if he was less than willing to share anything, much less any medical data.

"Well, she's not," he informed them stiffly. "So unless there's another specific reason why you're here—"

"There is," Chris said, interrupting him before Rowe could tell them to leave.

The thin lips drew back into an amazingly wide frown. "Oh joy," the man declared, his voice indicating that his feelings reflected anything but.

Chris pushed on as if he'd taken no notice of the ME's sarcastic tone. "I was hoping that the preliminary report on Bethany Miller was completed."

"Hope, such a frail word," Dr. Rowe commented cynically.

Suzie found herself taking an instant dislike to the man. O'Bannon might have irritated her, but there was no reason for the medical examiner to be so rude to him. She took offense for the detective. O'Bannon was just doing his job. There was no need to be so waspish with him—or her by association, since she was, after all, partnered up with Chris.

"We'd like to see the preliminary report on the current victim because it might help us ascertain if this is the work of a serial killer," Suzie told the older man, cutting in.

Eyes like small black marbles, perpetually moving, took measure of her over the top of his glasses. "And who might you be? Another privileged Cavanaugh?" He made no effort to hide the sneer in his voice or on his face as he mentioned the name.

"I'm CSI Susannah Quinn," she informed the ME, who was just barely taller than she was. "And I work for Sean Cavanaugh, who's in charge of the day shift at the crime lab. He also happens to be the chief of detectives' brother. Any other credentials you need to hear before you answer our questions?" she asked sharply.

Out of the corner of her eye, she saw the approving grin on Chris's face, but pretended not to.

Outnumbered, the ME frowned more deeply. It was apparent that he knew he had to give in, but made it clear he wasn't happy about it.

"I think I've got the report here somewhere," he said coldly.

Since it was right on top of his desk, Rowe couldn't pretend to shuffle papers, looking for the report, for very long. With an annoyed huff, he slapped the folder holding the report in front of Chris.

"Did you find any skin under her nails?" Chris asked him.

Rowe gave him a withering glance. "It's all right there in the report," he stated. "I'm assuming you can read. Or do you need it read to you?"

Suzie pulled the folder from beneath the man's hand. His belittling attitude toward O'Bannon was really beginning to aggravate her. She felt her temper rising, in part because she had no desire to feel so protective of the detective. There was no reason for it. They weren't even partners, only *temporary* ones. And yet she wanted to put Rowe in his place.

"We'll take it from here," she informed the ME, all but snarling the words.

Doing her best to calm down, Suzie counted to ten as they walked out of the autopsy room. "That man has a serious attitude problem," she said, glaring over her shoulder when they reached the hall.

Chris laughed shortly. "Welcome to my world."

She looked at him as they neared the elevator. "You mean because you're a Cavanaugh?" She'd never thought about that side of it. Never assumed that there was a downside to being a member of that family.

He pressed the elevator call button. "Don't get me wrong. Most of the time it's pretty great. The generation before me carved out some really nice niches and created a lot of respect for the rest of us. Not to mention that Uncle Andrew throws some damn good parties. And on occasion, because of our connection, some of us might have availed ourselves of a few shortcuts here and there—all in the line of duty for the greater good," he was quick to add, thinking of his last visit to Valri to get the benefit of her rather incredibly extensive computer expertise.

"But there are people on the force who dislike anyone named or related to a Cavanaugh for the very things I mentioned. And those people are never going to be brought around, no matter what any of us do to try and make them see that we're all on the same team. That we're just hardworking, decent people like they are."

"I know," Suzie acknowledged quietly, remembering how people had turned on her family once what her father had done became public knowledge. Everything she had held dear was ripped away from her. Even the people who didn't turn on her couldn't believe that she hadn't known what her father was up to—which made her, her brother and her mother accessories after the fact.

It seemed no one could believe that they had been duped like the rest of the town. That had hurt most of all. There were times when she felt that was even more heartbreaking than being betrayed by the father she had so blindly worshipped.

"You 'know?'" Chris repeated, somewhat mystified. There'd been a glimmer of something in her voice, but he couldn't pin it down. So instead, he teased her. "Are you a closet Cavanaugh?" he asked with a laugh.

Suzie roused herself. "No. I mean, I can sympathize what you're going through," she said dismissively.

It was more than that, Chris thought. He'd definitely seen something in her eyes, just for a moment. It wasn't sympathy, more like empathy. Like someone who knew what it was like to have been on the receiving end of envy. Or hate.

Despite his claim to preferring to get information firsthand, Chris decided that he needed to do a little digging into CSI Susannah Quinn's background. The pile of questions he had about her was mounting.

He wanted answers.

Realizing that their conversation had been left dangling, he tied up the ends. "Thanks," he said, to her proclamation of sympathy.

They got on the empty elevator. He was still holding the folder she'd given him.

"Are you going to read that report or just carry it around?" she asked, trying to change the subject. She didn't want him asking her any questions or probing into her life, and he had that look in his eyes that made her leery.

"I see our bonding moment is over," he noted. "Since we've got some time to kill before happy hour, let's go up to squad room to read this and do a little research on the internet."

"Happy hour?" she questioned. Was he talking about going out drinking? When had she given him any indication that she wanted to be included in that? The last thing she wanted was to socialize with him after hours.

He nodded. "That's when we go to The Saint to see if Sellers's alibi holds up. According to what he said, that's when his cronies will be there."

"What if he gets there ahead of us to coach the bartender and his friends?" Suzie asked. "For all we know, Sellers might have just given us a list of people he knew were always there around this time, and he'd be going to go to the bar to tell them to say he was there on Sunday."

"Good point," Chris agreed. She was giving Sellers's guilt a lot of thought. Had she changed her mind? "But I thought you were the one who didn't think he was guilty."

"I don't, but anything's possible," she told the detective. "Making sure that Sellers's story is actually on the level is just covering all the bases."

Chris laughed. He liked the way her mind worked. "Damn, no wonder Uncle Sean is so impressed with you," he told her.

"He just makes working easy."

And so do you, Suzie Q, Chris thought. *At least, easy on the eyes.*

Having lifted Sellers's picture from a copy of his driver's license online, Chris used that to show the bartender, after the man had seen their credentials and badges.

"Was this man here on Sunday night?" Chris asked.

The bartender took one glance at the photo Chris had put on the counter. "Yeah, and I wish he wasn't."

Chris took the photo and replaced it into his wallet. "We were under the impression that he spends a lot of money drinking here."

"He does, but he also brings the place down," the bartender complained. He smiled at Suzie. "Every night, Sellers is here, going on and on about how this hot model chick broke his heart."

"And he was here Sunday night?" Chris questioned. "You're sure?"

The guy went back to polishing the counter. The surface was dull, but buffed clean. "I'm sure. After a while, the other customers asked me to turn up the sound on the game that was on that night, to drown him out."

"You have any security cameras here?" Chris asked, looking around the rather small area. He didn't see any, but that didn't mean they weren't around.

"Not in the place," the bartender admitted, "but I have one right outside the door. I got it for security reasons, in case there's a robbery. There's one facing the alley, as well." He stopped buffing to think. "If you're interested, you could probably see Sellers coming in and then leaving sometime later. I had to call him an Uber, then help him into it."

Suzie exchanged looks with Chris. "An Uber?" she questioned. "Why? Sellers lives within walking distance of this place."

"According to him he does, but Sunday he wasn't in any condition to walk," the bartender told them. "Don't get me wrong, I feel sorry for the guy. But there's just so much carrying on people can take. Personally, I hope he buys himself a bottle and just stays home, drinking, until he's got this thing out of his system." He looked at the two of them, his curiosity obviously aroused. "Why are you asking all these questions about Sellers? Something happen to him?" As if realizing that his last statement might have been taken in the wrong light, he quickly told them, "I wasn't serious about wanting him to stay away."

"We're just trying to verify something," Chris answered noncommittally. "Mind if we see the feed on the security camera?"

Still looking somewhat concerned that he might have misspoken, the bartender beckoned them to his back office. "No problem," he said obligingly.

"Well, I guess that puts the brokenhearted ex-boyfriend in the clear," Chris said when they finally left The Saint.

Suzie got into the passenger side of his vehicle. "There's nothing helpful in the preliminary autopsy report, either." There was a note of frustration in her voice as she buckled up.

About to start the car, Chris looked at her. Something wasn't making sense to him. "When did you read the autopsy report?"

"While you were driving to The Saint."

He'd noticed her flipping through the report, but he hadn't thought she'd read it thoroughly. "You read the whole thing?" he questioned now.

"Yes."

"But it was about a ten-minute drive from the precinct to the bar," he said. The preliminary report was about ten pages long, with a lot of medical jargon. Single-spaced. How could she read so fast?

"It wasn't exactly *War and Peace*," she pointed out. And then, because she sensed he was waiting for more, she told him, "I speed-read."

"Of course you do," he said. The woman was one surprise after another. "Anything else about you I should know?"

"I think you know enough."

He hadn't even begun to scratch the surface. There was a lot more to Susannah Quinn than met the eye.

"That is a matter of opinion."

Was she going to have trouble with this man, after all? This was what she got for allowing her guard to drop temporarily.

"All right," she amended. "Let's put it this way. You know enough for us to work this case together."

Chris sincerely doubted that, but there was no point in arguing with her about it. He had a feeling he wouldn't win. This was going to take strategy—and sneakiness. "All right, why don't you tell me what was in the report."

A whole lot of nothing, she couldn't help thinking. Obliging him, she recited what she had read. "There was nothing underneath her fingernails, no traces of any kind of fiber on her anywhere. Time of death was estimated to be sometime between 11:00 p.m. and 3:00 a.m. And she was strangled—from behind.

According to the report, there was more pressure applied to the left side of her neck than the right. That means—"

"That the killer was most likely left-handed," Chris said.

She nodded. That was the only piece of information in the whole report that might give them something to work with. "That's something. I think," she qualified.

"Well, since only ten percent of the population is left-handed, that does shrink the suspect pool—in a manner of speaking," he said, then reminded her, "Sellers is right-handed."

"I know," she said with a sigh. The man was conclusively ruled out. Which brought them back to square one. "So where do we go from here?"

He stopped at a red light. It was his third in a row. This time of day, traffic trickled rather than moved. "Why don't we take a closer look at your serial killer theory?"

"It's not my theory," she protested.

If something went wrong with this investigation, she didn't want to risk him blaming her for it—even though she was strongly leaning in that direction. She was just worried that her personal experience was coloring her viewpoint.

"Okay, let's take a closer look at the possibility of this being the work of a serial killer," Chris rephrased, putting the theory in more general terms. "Does that satisfy you?"

Now he was talking down to her. "You don't have to humor me," she told him.

"Then what *do* I have to do to get on the right side of you?" he asked, throwing up his hands.

"Why would you want to get on the right side of me?" Suzie questioned. She was nothing to him. There was no reason for them to be in harmony.

"Because it makes working together a hell of a lot easier," Chris pointed out. Then he sighed. "Damn, but you are high maintenance."

She thought of herself as the exact opposite. "No, I'm not."

"Okay," he said, playing along. "Your evil twin is high maintenance."

She could see the barely contained annoyance just beneath the surface. Maybe she had been pushing too hard. He was, after all, attempting to be even-handed with her, and she did appreciate that.

"Sorry."

"Don't be sorry," he told her, "just do us both a favor and relax a little, because given half a chance, you are a damn good investigator. You've just got this baggage you keep tripping over."

Her eyes widened. Up until the last sentence, he'd been complimentary, and she'd considered relenting. But now she was worried. Did O'Bannon know? Had he somehow found out about her father? And who else knew?

She could feel her stomach tightening.

"I don't have baggage," she protested strongly.

"Okay," he allowed, then reworded his observation. "This invisible elephant you keep tripping over. Whatever it is, get rid of it, get over it, just get it out of your way, okay?" he implored. Having gotten that out of his system, he said, "Now, it's getting late and I'm hungry, so why don't we grab a bite to eat and then call it a night?"

She waved away his suggestion. "That's okay, I don't—"

"Eat?" he guessed. "Yeah, you do," he contradicted. "I've seen you, remember?"

She frowned slightly. He kept jumping in, substituting words for what she wanted to say. "I was going to mention that I don't mix my personal life with my professional one."

Chris laughed shortly. "From what I've seen, Suzie Q, you don't *have* a personal life to mix with anything. And just so you know, I'm proposing dinner, not marriage, so stop coming up with all these excuses, and grab dinner with me, okay?" He spared her a quick look. "I promise that's the only thing I'll grab."

She drew herself up. "I'm not afraid of you."

"Good, because I'm afraid enough of you for the both of us," he cracked. "So have dinner with me and calm my fears."

She couldn't help it; he made her laugh. Suzie shook her head. "You are crazy, you know that?"

"Well," he said honestly, "if I wasn't at the start of this week, I'm certainly getting there now."

She sat up, alert, as she saw their workplace out of

the corner of her eye. "You're passing the precinct," she told him as she watched it go by.

"The restaurant's not in the precinct," he answered simply.

Suzie sighed and sat back in her seat. "I give up."

"Good," he approved. "Surrender. I like that. You'll chew better if your jaw's not clenched."

Maybe she'd been too hasty in agreeing to partner up with this man.

The feeling in her gut concurred.

Chapter 10

Suzie was having second thoughts about agreeing to this. She would be better off just going home, not going to some restaurant with this detective who was much too confident for her own good.

"You really don't need to do this," she told Chris as he pulled up in front of what she assumed was a restaurant. It looked to be hardly more than a storefront, really. If it sat more than ten customers, she would be greatly surprised.

"Eat?" he asked, pulling up the hand brake and getting out. "Yeah, I do. I do it every day." After waiting for her to get out, he locked the vehicle and came around to her side. "It's kind of gotten to be a habit."

"No, I mean bring me here."

"You've got to eat, too, Suzie Q. You've got to keep your strength up." He held the door open for her.

She had no choice but to enter the restaurant. She was right: the place was tiny. But it did have a warmth to it, she grudgingly admitted. "Why? So I can put up with you?"

Taking her arm, Chris guided her over to a table.

Apparently, the restaurant was self-seating, she thought.

"I was going to say to go on with the investigation," he answered, "but you can have it your way if it makes you happy."

Sitting down across from him at the table, she met his gaze. "What would make me happy is to go home."

He appeared completely unconvinced, then went on to tell her why. "I don't think you mean that. Home's a dark and lonely place. You probably have nothing in the refrigerator and there's a three-quarters-empty box of stale breakfast cereal in your pantry."

She resented that he thought he knew her so well. "You're wrong on both counts," she informed him.

Obligingly, Chris reversed the order. "Okay, your pantry's empty and the cereal's in your refrigerator?" he guessed.

She didn't want him digging into her life and definitely not into her head. "Maybe your time would be better spent figuring out who killed our victim and why," she told the detective in a voice that was meant to cut him dead.

"Already working on it," he answered, with a cheerful confidence she found both annoying and yet somehow strangely compelling.

"All right," she challenged, not sure if she believed him. "Fill me in." Listening to dull details about the investigation had to be better than feeling herself being dissected by those penetrating green eyes of his.

"It's kind of sketchy," Chris admitted.

A sense of satisfaction washed over her. He had nothing, and ultimately, was all talk. "Uh-huh. Thought so."

"But tomorrow," he went on, pretending not to notice the smug look on her face, "I thought we could track down and talk to a few of those people we managed to identify in the videos."

"Who?" she questioned. At last count, as far as she knew, there'd been only two people that he'd identified. "Besides Warren Eldridge and Simon Silas?"

"Those two, to start," he allowed.

"And that's all we've got?" Suzie asked, confident that she already knew the answer. The videos had been too grainy for her to positively identify those two, but he seemed to be certain that Eldridge and Silas were in that clip.

Chris meted out his words slowly, as if doing so gave them more weight. He seemed pleased to prove her wrong. "Actually, no. A few more of the attendees were identified."

She'd gotten eyestrain looking at those videos and

come away not being able to see anyone clearly. "By who?" she asked.

He laughed. It had taken a lot of pleading on his part, as well as calling in some favors.

"Let's just say that I owe my cousin Valri my firstborn. And Brenda gets the second one," he added after a beat.

"Brenda?" Suzie repeated. And then it occurred to her who he might be talking about. "You don't mean the head of the tech lab, do you?"

The look on his face told her that he got a kick out of her wording. "Why wouldn't I?"

"Right." What was she thinking? "She's a Cavanaugh, too," Suzie realized.

He raised another important point. "Don't forget she's also the chief of d's daughter-in-law," he reminded her, then replayed her last sentence. "But you say that as if it's a bad thing, being a Cavanaugh. As a detective, I'm supposed to use everything in my skill set to solve a crime. Access to the more capable people in the family *is* part of my skill set," he told her.

She sighed, shaking her head. "Who am I to argue?"

"I don't know, but you've been doing a damn good job of it so far," he commented. "Why don't we call a truce and order?" he suggested. "The sooner we eat, the sooner you can get rid of me," he added.

"Waitress!" Suzie called out in response, raising her hand to attract the attention of the lone server, who had just passed their table.

"You sure know how to make a guy feel special," he told her, amused.

She refused to see his comment in any light that had the possibility of making her feel uncomfortable. "You're not a guy, you're just a detective I'm working with. *Temporarily*."

"*Just* a detective?" he echoed. "I'm a man just like any other man. If you prick us, do we not bleed? If you kill us, do we not die?" he asked her, deliberately paraphrasing lines from one of Shakespeare's more famous plays.

Susie's eyes narrowed. "Don't tempt me to test that theory and find out."

"Wait, I saw a smile," Chris declared triumphantly. "It's a little one, but it's there. I knew it," he cried. "I'm growing on you."

Damn it, she hadn't meant to smile. She was certain she'd kept a straight face. The problem was, he did amuse her—to an extent.

"Don't pat yourself on the back just yet, O'Bannon. Fungus grows on things, too."

The overworked waitress picked that moment to finally come over to their table. "What can I get for you?" she asked, an inviting smile on her face. She was looking at Suzie first.

"An escape route." The words just slipped out.

The waitress in turn looked confused. "Excuse me?"

Rather than backtrack, Suzie placed her order. "I'll have the chicken parmesan."

"My favorite," the young woman commented, nodding in approval. "And how would you like that?"

There was no hesitation on Suzie's part. "Quickly."

Chris felt compelled to intercede. "This is our first date," he told the waitress with a wink. "She's in a hurry to get back to my place."

"I don't blame her," the woman responded, a wistful note in her voice as she looked enviously at Suzie. "And your order, sir?"

In the interest of speed, he kept it simple. "I'll have what she's having."

"Two chicken parmesans coming up," the young woman told them, making the proper notations. "Oh, and if it doesn't turn out," she told Chris, lowering her voice, "call me." She left a card on the table in front of him.

Picking up the card, Chris slipped it into his pocket. He didn't want to take a chance on insulting the waitress.

"See?" he said. "Not everyone finds me repulsive, Suzie Q."

"You do know I'm carrying a gun," she reminded him pointedly.

His smile only widened. "That's what makes it so exciting."

Suzie rolled her eyes.

"There, that wasn't so bad, was it?" Chris asked an hour later as he and Suzie finally left the restaurant.

She felt very full, but in a pleasant way. She

couldn't remember feeling this well fed in a long time. "I hate to admit it, but it was excellent. I'm talking about the food," she added, when it suddenly occurred to her that he would think she was referring to the conversation over dinner.

"Never thought you meant anything else," Chris told her innocently.

He'd said it with a straight face, but his tone of voice made her think he really *didn't* mean the food.

She took a deep breath of the heavier night air. She felt too full to walk any great distance, so she looked at Chris. "You are going to drive me back to my car in the police parking lot, aren't you?"

He left it up to her. "Unless there's somewhere else you want to go."

"No, absolutely not," she told him in no uncertain terms. "I want to get back to my car."

"Then that's where I'll take you," he answered.

They got into his car and he threaded his way out onto the main drag.

Glancing in Suzie's direction, he noticed that she was still as stiff as he'd ever seen her. What was going on in her head?

"Relax, I'm not part of some international kidnapping ring grabbing up women in the street and selling them into slavery. Even if I was," he told her, "I'd lose my standing bringing you in. You'd flatten them all within a couple of hours."

"You make me sound like some kind of cavewoman."

"Not at all." Although she could be his cavewoman anytime, he thought, keeping the comment to himself. He wasn't about to risk her taking his head off and handing it to him. "Just a very worthy opponent. Lord knows I'd hate to be on the wrong side of you."

"What makes you think you're not?" she challenged.

"Remember those skill sets I mentioned?" he asked her. "Well, I'm using part of them right now. They help me read people, and I can read you." He grinned at her confidentially. "You're having trouble keeping that guard up against me."

He was getting too close for her comfort and she needed to keep him at arm's distance. "Are all the Cavanaughs of your generation so cocky?" she asked.

They were back in the police parking lot and he came to a stop. "The lucky ones are," he told her, and then pointed out, in case it escaped her, "I brought you back safe and sound—and fed—just like I promised."

That was when Suzie finally looked at the vehicle on her right. The one he'd just pulled up beside. Her eyes widened.

"How did you know this was my car?" she asked. To the best of her recollection, he hadn't seen her driving it or parking it.

"I'm a detective," he answered with a broad grin. "I detect." Before she could say anything in response, he said, "Go home and get some sleep, Suzie Q. And come back more trusting in the morning." And then he couldn't keep himself from adding, "I'm not such a bad guy."

"Jury's still out on that," she told him as she got out, then closed his car door behind her.

The problem was, Suzie thought as she got into her own vehicle, that jury she'd just so flippantly evoked was turning on her.

To get an early start on searching for similar, unsolved cases in the last five years, Suzie came into the precinct a little after seven. She expected to find the squad room empty, and it was—except for one occupant.

The last person she would have expected to find there.

Approaching the desk she'd been assigned to, the one, she believed, that belonged to the partner O'Bannon had told her was off on sick leave, she pulled out the chair and sat down. All the while never taking her eyes from the other figure in the squad room: O'Bannon.

"What are you doing here?" she asked him, not bothering to hide her surprise.

Chris was wearing different clothes than yesterday. Otherwise she would have thought that maybe he'd gone to meet some of his fellow detectives at Malone's, the cop bar only a few blocks from the precinct, then come back to the squad room to sleep it off at his desk.

To her, that would have been a more plausible

explanation for finding him here at this hour of the morning.

"I think they call it working—but don't quote me," Chris warned wryly. Finally looking up, he said, "You look surprised."

She was. There was no point in pretending otherwise. No one was that good of an actress. "I thought you were the type to come in late."

"Well, you're wrong," he pointed out, then added, "There're a lot of things about me you might have gotten wrong." He'd been at it for a while now and could do with a break. "Why don't you grab some coffee and I'll fill you in on what I've found so far?"

"Tea," she corrected, knowing it was a petty point. It didn't stop her. "I drink tea."

"Okay, then grab some tea," he said, "and I'll fill you in on what I've found so far."

"The hell with the tea," Suzie declared, dragging her chair around so that she could position it next to his. "Fill me in now."

He liked her eagerness. A small part of him couldn't help but wonder what it would be like to have that eagerness focused on him.

"You know that idea you had about a serial killer? Well, you just might be onto something. I went through all the unsolved cases in the Northern California region with similar MOs in the last ten years. Then I widened my search to include Southern California, as well."

"And?" she pressed, almost afraid to hear what he had to say. Either way it would be bad. He'd either found no similar MOs, which meant they were back to that awful square one again, or he'd found a number of such cases, which meant some bloodthirsty psychopath was out there, killing women for pleasure and sport.

It felt like a lose-lose situation.

"And," Chris was saying, "I found nine. Nine women who were strangled. Nine young, statuesque blondes," he elaborated, "who just disappeared without a trace—until their bodies were found in abandoned buildings.

"Since they were all in different cities throughout the state, no one made the connection between these women." He looked at Suzie with amazement. "You were right," he declared.

"I didn't want to be," she answered in almost a whisper.

He understood exactly where she was coming from. "Yeah, I know. As grim as it sounds, one body is a lot easier to deal with than the thought of nine bodies."

"*If* there's only nine," she qualified.

When he gazed at her quizzically, she explained, "There might have been more, but maybe they weren't found. Not every abandoned building gets made over into something else, so it's possible that the dead women don't get discovered. In some places, buildings stay empty and abandoned for years. The only reason Bethany was found was because those two teens were scavenging for whatever souvenirs might have been left over after that impromptu bash. If they hadn't done that, who knows?" she said. "There's been no missing person's report filed on Bethany. Neither her ex-boyfriend nor her ex-roommate were looking for her. It's possible that might have been the case with other victims, as well."

"What are you suggesting?" he asked. "That those victims were wined and dined to death? Or maybe they were lured away with the promise of a lifetime of parties and a lavish lifestyle?"

"To be honest," Suzie confessed, "I don't know yet." She paused, thinking. "Maybe the killer has a thing against tall, beautiful young blondes. Or maybe he was dumped by one, like Sellers? Or maybe killing these beautiful women with their whole lives in front of them fills some inner bloodlust for the killer," she said, more to herself than to Chris, adding under her breath, "He's probably not doing it to get them to atone for their lives of sin."

Chris looked at her sharply, not quite sure he heard her correctly. "What?"

Suzie blinked. Damn it, she had to watch herself more carefully. But there was so much here that kept reminding her of her father's spree.

She shook her head. "Nothing."

But Chris *had* heard her and he replayed her words in his mind now. "Where did that come from?" he asked.

Denial would just make O'Bannon more insistent, she knew that, so she soft-pedaled what she'd said. "I'm just throwing things out there."

"Well, that last thing was right out of left field."

"That's what 'throwing' is all about," she said flippantly.

"You've had experience with this kind of thing before?" Chris questioned.

"No," she snapped. "Now stop asking *me* questions and let's get back to this killer and what we know about him. I'll make a list," she decided, pulling out a sheet of paper. She looked for a pen.

And what do I know about you, Suzie Q? he couldn't help wondering.

Their killer wasn't the only mystery here.

Chapter 11

Looking back, Chris thought of the day as being less than productive. He felt that the bulk of it was spent spinning wheels and going nowhere, since he and Suzie were predominatly talking with people who had no desire to talk. At least, not about an impromptu bash where a dead body was discovered.

Consequently, interviewing the handful of people who had been identified on the two somewhat brief, grainy cell phone videos that had been taken of the partygoers proved to be every bit as fruitless as Suzie had predicted.

It wasn't that Chris minded her being right. He was just disappointed that it had to be about something as vital as this.

To make matters worse, each of the people they

eventually interviewed had been difficult to track down. And once this handful of possible witnesses were cornered one by one, they proved to be unwilling to even admit that they had attended the so-called secret bash. When they did, reluctantly, own up to having been there "briefly," not one would admit that they saw Bethany Miller there.

"Take a closer look," Chris urged a stockbroker named Jonah Hayes. Hayes definitely did not appear happy to have two members of the Aurora Police Department in his office, questioning him.

If Hayes actually looked at the photograph placed on his desk, his glance had to have been quicker than the speed of light, Suzie judged.

"No," he insisted, turning his head away. "I said no, I've never seen this woman."

Suzie moved the photograph so that it was in his line of vision again. "Picture her alive," she prompted in a steely voice. "With color in her face."

"No," the broker said adamantly. "I *don't know her*." Hayes squared his rather sloping shoulders. "Now please leave or I'll be forced to call Security." To underscore his threat, he reached for the phone on his desk.

Unfazed, Chris asked him, "Does your boss know that you like to attend floating bashes in abandoned buildings?"

Hayes left the phone receiver where it was. Even so, he gave it one more try. "I don't know what you're talking about."

"Oh, I think you do," Chris told him. "We have you on video. Your boss might enjoy seeing it."

He instantly went on the defensive. "What's on it?" the broker asked, looking rather spooked about the existence of a video.

"What are you afraid is on it?" Suzie asked, boxing him in. "Maybe you were doing something you shouldn't have been?" she suggested.

Seeing that Hayes was rattled, Chris was quick to press their advantage. "You do realize that you were trespassing," he assumed. "That means you were there illegally."

Hayes really seemed nervous now. "Nobody said anything about illegal," he cried. "Besides, the people who were running this bash, they were all big shots. Men who are on the boards of at least a dozen charitable organizations. Men who don't worry about minor rules being bent." Hayes was throwing up reasons like hurdles in an Olympic race.

"Minor rules," Chris echoed. "You mean like murder?" he asked, bending over the man's chair, talking into his face.

Obviously frightened, Hayes cowered. "Nobody was murdered," he cried.

"Then how do you explain her?" Suzie asked, pushing the photograph back in front of him.

"I don't," Hayes answered helplessly. "Look, you've got to believe me." He was pleading now. "I never saw her."

"Why do we have to believe you?" Chris demanded.

Hayes was coming apart. "Because it's true! Look, a lot of other people were there besides me. Why don't you talk to some of them? Maybe they saw her—but I *didn't*. I swear I didn't!"

"All right," Chris said, playing along, "give us some names. Who else was at this thing?"

Hayes abruptly stopped talking. Several seconds passed as he looked from the detective to the crime scene investigator, not volunteering anyone's name.

"I see you're having a lapse of memory," Chris observed. "Maybe a trip to the station and a few hours in a holding cell might jar that for you," he told the broker gamely.

Panic entered the stockbroker's dark eyes. "All right, all right, I'll give you names. But you can't tell them I told you."

Chris gave him a boy scout salute. "Your secret's safe with us," he promised.

"But if any of these people say they remember seeing you with this woman, we're coming back for you," Suzie told the broker.

Hayes rattled off the names, swearing again that he had never seen Bethany Miller, alive *or* dead.

"I don't know about you, but I'm bushed," Chris said to Suzie some ten hours later. The time had been filled with more spinning wheels, and they had gotten no further than where they'd been when they began. "I never saw so many people with such short-term memories in my life," he complained.

Suzie had grown even quieter than usual in the

last hour. She'd been working on a theory. "There is another explanation."

Chris had all but collapsed in the driver's seat. Starting the car took effort. He felt as if his limbs were filled with lead. "What, they're all in collusion?"

"No," she replied. "Our victim was never at the bash in the first place." Chris looked at her sharply. Suzie continued. "Just because Bethany was found on the premises doesn't mean that she was there while the party was in progress."

Chris began to speak, but Suzie held her hand up, as if to physically hold back his words. "We've already established that she was killed elsewhere. Maybe Bethany started out 'elsewhere' and never got a chance to actually attend this bash."

She could see that O'Bannon was skeptical, so she pressed on. "Think about it," she urged. "Yes, Bethany looks like a lot of other beautiful blondes in California—it's practically a prerequisite in order to live here," she cracked, aware that she was a blonde herself. "But you have to admit that even among beautiful blondes, she was still pretty outstanding. One of those people we talked to today would have had to remember seeing her—*if* she'd been there to be seen."

"I suppose that makes sense," Chris said, rolling the idea over in his mind. "But then, if she hadn't been there to begin with, why leave her at the site of the bash?"

Suzie didn't have an answer for that—yet. "Hey, I

came up with most of the explanation. You can come up with that part."

"Oh, yeah, the easy part," Chris acknowledged with a touch of sarcasm.

She shrugged innocently. "Can't do all your work for you, O'Bannon."

When they got back to the precinct, Chris looked down at the list of attendees on his desk. It was comprised of the people Valri and Brenda had wound up identifying on the videos, plus the names they had gotten from Hayes. The people they had talked to today had either given them the same names, or had been, in their words, "too wasted to notice anybody."

They'd gotten only halfway through it, and right now, the list looked daunting.

"What do you say to calling it a night and going through the rest of this—" Chris nodded toward the sheet "—first thing tomorrow?"

"Sounds like a plan to me," Suzie agreed. For once she was too tired to argue with him.

Chris was already up on his feet. "C'mon, I'll walk you out."

Even tired, she still balked. "This is a police building. I don't need an escort."

Why did everything turn into an argument with this woman? Did she even *know* how not to argue? he wondered. "Maybe I do," he replied.

She sighed. "C'mon." She beckoned for him to

follow her as she headed for the door. "Does your family know how weird you are?"

"They have their suspicions," he told her with a smile.

Crossing the threshold into the hall, she murmured, "Remind me to send your mother flowers."

"She'd like that," he said cheerfully.

Suzie just shook her head.

The next day proved to be just as unproductive as the first.

On the third day, they reached the end of the list, with no breakthroughs, major or otherwise.

"Got an idea," Chris announced.

"Are you asking me or telling me?" Suzie retorted.

"Telling you, but if you've got one, I'm open to it," he said.

"I've got nothing," she admitted rather ruefully, far from happy to be coming up empty.

"Let's try something else, then," he suggested. "Let's revisit those nine murder victims with similar MOs that we uncovered the other day."

"Revisit how, specifically?" she asked.

"We'll talk to the investigating detective assigned to each case," he said, for the time being unable to think of any other course of action to take. "See how many similarities we can come up with. Unless you've got a better idea," he qualified.

She wondered if he was as generous as he came across, or if there was some other reason behind his being seemingly open to anything she had to contribute. Was he just trying to get her off guard? And if so, why? Was the man up to something?

"No, that seems like a very good idea to me," she told him.

Some of the detectives they wound up talking to were grateful for any new input they might have on their case, and were intrigued that the working theory now was that the murders might be the work of a serial killer.

Other detectives blatantly resented the intrusion from a different police department.

Still others had declared the investigation they'd once handled to be a cold case. Which meant they had just walked away from the murder as if it had never happened.

For the most part, dishearteningly, Chris and Suzie found dead ends. But in a few instances there were glaring similarities beyond the dead women's once breathtaking looks.

"You know, now that you mention it, there was talk about this 'unofficial' bash taking place the night of the murder," Detective Jack Webster, an old-timer a hairbreadth away from retirement, told them when they asked him about a cold case he had handled. "I remember a couple of people I interviewed bragging that more than a thousand people attended the bash and that it went on for over two days."

"Where?" Chris asked. "Do you remember where they said it took place?"

The sloped shoulders rose and fell beneath a

checkered sport coat. "Only place that could hold that many people would be the Eldridge Center."

"Come again?" Chris asked, then reminded the detective, "We're not from around here."

"It's a performance venue," Webster explained. "Around the time that this girl's body was found, there were rumors that the center, which was being renovated at the time… Ownership had just changed hands," he added as a sidebar. "Anyway, there were rumors that there was some big bash being held there. We only found out about it after the fact. Couldn't find all that many people who would actually admit to being there. It was like this big, inside secret. You know, like a frat party—except that the men there were a lot older than your average frat boy," he told them with a sigh. It was obvious that the case had frustrated him in its time.

"The girl—did her family come forward to claim her?" Suzie asked.

"Another sad story," Webster admitted. "The victim had no ID on her. Her fingerprints weren't on file in the system and DNA testing was in its infancy, so the whole thing just died there."

"You think that maybe you could run a test now?" Chris suggested.

Webster shook his head, his expression rueful. "I'm afraid that money's kind of tight around here."

"We could do it," Suzie volunteered, surprising her partner. "We'll take chain of custody of the evidence—anything you had by way of her DNA—and do the test in our lab in Aurora."

"That's kind of unorthodox," Chris began, attempting to talk her out of her offer.

But Suzie wasn't going to be dissuaded. "If there's a problem, I can pay for it out of my own pocket," she told Chris.

That was good enough for Webster, who they could see was anticipating another closed case being added to his final tally. It would be viewed as a nice send-off.

"Sure, I'll have Evidence sign it over to you," the detective told them.

"Why is this case so important to you?" Chris asked her when they were finally back in his vehicle and returning from Oakridge to Aurora.

"Someone could still be waiting for that girl to walk through the door," Suzie told him, adding with feeling, "They deserve answers."

There was more to it than that and they both knew it, Chris thought. For a moment, he debated letting it go, just as he had a number of times before. But he found that he couldn't.

"Suzie, what happened to you?" he asked her. There was sympathy as well as curiosity in his voice.

Walls instantly went up. "What do you mean?" she asked stiffly.

He called it the way he saw it, without sugarcoating it. "You're almost obsessed with finding the killer—over and above the usual zeal for solving a case. Is this personal for you?"

There was anger in her eyes when she looked at

him. "Young women are being slaughtered by a monster. He could be eyeing his next victim right now. It should be personal to everyone."

She wasn't going to tell him. There was no point in agitating her any further. She didn't trust him enough, he decided.

"Uncle," he cried.

Suzie stared at him, confused. "What?"

"I give up," he explained. "You know, 'uncle.'"

Suzie sighed. She wasn't into word games. They weren't part of her makeup or background. "Why don't you just say that I'm right instead of resorting to code words?"

The only way he was going to get anywhere with her was by saying "You're right." And then he paused. In her zeal, a very pertinent point seemed to have escaped Suzie. "You also know that in order for the lab to get anywhere with making an ID using the girl's DNA, they're going have to have something to compare that DNA to, right?"

He was talking down to her again, she thought. "I know that. I'm not an idiot, O'Bannon."

"Never crossed my mind," he told her. "So what's the plan?"

She knew what he was asking her. The answer was simple. The execution was not. "We pull up any missing person's reports that were filed nine years ago."

He could just see someone in Accounting getting ready to do battle with the petite firebrand in the passenger seat. "This might turn out to be pricey."

She shrugged. "I have a bank account and nothing to spend it on."

She had to be kidding, he thought. One look at her face told him she wasn't. "I could come up with some suggestions," he told her.

"I'm sure you could," she replied, "but I'm not interested in them."

"Cold, Suzie Q," he pronounced. "Cold."

"Drive faster," she instructed. They were on the open road and he was going just under the speed limit. "We need to get back to the precinct so I can get started finding those missing person's reports."

"Not to throw cold water on your plans," he said, knowing he was doing just that, "but there might not be one for the victim."

She recalled that her father had made a point of eliminating young women who had no families to look for them or mourn for them. It was one of the "perks" of being a volunteer at the homeless shelter. Suzie was well aware that the murder victim might not have had anyone file a missing person's report on her, but nevertheless, she could still hope.

"Right now, I'd rather you didn't rain on my parade, O'Bannon."

He grinned at her. "I wouldn't dream of it," Chris said.

"By the way," he began, after they'd driven in silence for a good twenty minutes or so, "the family's having a get-together this Saturday."

That was out of left field, she thought. "What family?"

"My family."

"Oh." She supposed it made sense, his talking about his family. "Okay. Have fun."

"That's not the point."

That didn't make any sense to her. "Then why get together?"

"No, I mean that's not the point of why I'm telling you this." Before she could ask what was, he said, "You're invited."

That gave her pause for a moment and then she said, "Thank you."

Her response sounded oddly stilted to his ear, so he asked, "Then you'll come?"

She couldn't very well say she was coming when she knew she wasn't. She'd had more than her fill of lies in her lifetime.

"No."

"Then what are you thanking me for?"

"The invitation," she told him. "It's always nice to be invited to something."

If that was her reasoning, then why wouldn't she come? "But not to go?"

She shrugged. "Why spoil things?"

He was completely and utterly lost—and not embarrassed to tell her so. "I have no idea what goes through that mind of yours, but I think a family get-together might really do you some good."

How could he even think that? "Your family, not mine, remember?"

He was open to things, as he knew his uncle Andrew was. The man thrived on hospitality. “Then bring your family.”

“I don’t have a family.”

Even saying the words hurt. She saw an expression she took to be pity entering the detective’s eyes. Her back went up immediately.

“I mean, I have a brother,” she amended, “but he’s on the East Coast.” Not that they were close anymore, she thought. That had gone out the window when the scandal surrounding their father had broken. She kept holding out hope that there was some mistake. Her brother had turned on their father the moment the local police came to arrest him.

“All the more reason to come this Saturday,” Chris urged. “I promise you won’t regret it,” he told her warmly.

“We’ll see,” she said, thinking that should get him to stop. It was the politest way she knew to put Chris off.

“Okay, we will,” he agreed, sparing her a glance before he turned back to watching the open road. It sounded more like a promise than a throwaway phrase.

She had the uneasy feeling that maybe, despite her resolution, it wasn’t over, after all.

Chapter 12

"I think I've maybe finally found her," Suzie announced some five hours later, fingering the tiny gold cross around her neck. The one she never took off, because it was the last thing her mother had given her before their world imploded.

Her neck and shoulders were killing her. She'd been hunched over her computer, carefully reading all the missing person's reports that had been filed with different police departments throughout the state. They were all on young women who had been reported missing around the general time period that their coroner had estimated this particular Jane Doe had been killed.

It completely astonished Suzie that there were so

many missing young women between the ages of seventeen and thirty who had never been found.

"Good," Chris said, getting up from his computer and circling around to her desk to take a look at her screen. "Because I'm definitely getting blurred vision, going through all those old files." He shook his head, thinking of the reports he'd been reading. "Something's seriously wrong when so many girls go missing."

Suzie leaned back in her chair to allow him to get a better view of the report she had currently pulled up on her screen.

He read the description out loud. "'Cara Wilson, twenty-one, aspiring model. Blond, five-nine, 120 pounds.'" Chris stepped back. Although he didn't mind the close proximity to Suzie, he had a feeling she might have something to say about it. "So far, that could describe Bethany Miller," he commented.

Suzie didn't disagree. There was something eerily similar between the dead girls. She had a sick feeling that maybe this was the tip of the iceberg.

First things first, she reminded herself. She needed to identify Jane Doe.

"The report was filed by her mother. According to this, Cara's roommate said Cara took off for a party she was certain was going to be her 'ticket to the career she felt she was destined for.' The roommate, Jill Barnes, said that Cara told her she could come along, too, but Jill came down with food poisoning the afternoon before the party and couldn't go." Suzie had read and reread the report. She knew it by heart at this point. "Cara never came back."

Chris skimmed to the bottom of the report. "According to the investigating officer, the roommate had no idea where the party was being held, only that Cara said it was really ingenious." He looked at Suzie, not wanting to jump to conclusions. "Could mean anything."

Suzie had no such reservations. "Could also mean a 'floating party' like the one in the abandoned department store." She shifted her chair so that she was looking at Chris directly. "We could get some personal item from Cara's mother to compare to the unidentified dead girl's DNA."

He didn't want Suzie getting too excited yet. "Cara's mother might have moved."

Not if the woman was waiting for her daughter to come home, Suzie thought. "Well, we won't find out sitting here, will we?" she said, already on her feet and halfway to the door. "You don't have to come if you've got something else to do," she called over her shoulder.

As if he was going to sit here, twiddling his thumbs. "The hell I don't," Chris said, taking off after her.

Cara Wilson's mother, Amy, was a small, pale-faced woman who looked as if she might have once been very pretty, before all hope had been stripped from her. In her early fifties, for the last nine years

Amy Wilson had only been going through the motions of living.

"Yes?" she asked, when she opened the door of her modest, one-story house and gazed at them.

"Mrs. Wilson, I'm CSI Susannah Quinn and this is Detective Christian O'Bannon," Suzie told her, holding up her credentials and badge. Chris was doing the same. "We're with the Aurora Police Department. May we come in to talk with you?"

The woman continued holding the door ajar, looking at the duo uncertainly, as if she heard the words but didn't understand.

"Aurora?" she asked. "That's more than forty miles from here."

"Yes, ma'am, we know," Chris replied politely. Although they looked nothing alike, the woman somehow reminded him of his mother, the way she might have looked if something like this had happened to her. "But this might be about your daughter, Cara."

Rather than hope, dread instantly filled the woman's hazel eyes. "You found her?" she asked in a hushed whisper.

"To be quite honest, we're not sure, ma'am," Chris answered.

For a second, the woman looked as if she would sink to the floor right where she was standing. But then, one hand clutching the side of the door, she took a deep breath and said, "Please come in."

Opening the door all the way, Amy Wilson let them in. After she closed it, she led the way to her small, cheerless living room. Framed photographs of her daughter were displayed on every available surface within the room.

Although it was still daytime, no light seemed to be entering the living room. It was almost as if it wasn't allowed. Amy Wilson paused to turn on a lamp, but it was obvious that if she had been sitting in the room before they had come in, she had been sitting in darkness.

Perching on the edge of the sofa, she gestured for them to sit down on the love seat facing her, on the other side of the small, picture-cluttered coffee table. "How can I help?"

Suzie answered before Chris had a chance. "We need some personal item of Cara's so that we can match her DNA to—someone else's."

"To a victim's," Amy supplied grimly, her hands folded so tightly in her lap, her knuckles had gone white.

"Yes," Suzie told her.

"And then you'll know if it's her?" Amy asked almost hesitantly. "If it's my Cara?"

"And then we'll know," Suzie confirmed. She moved to the sofa to take the woman's hands in hers. She squeezed them tightly. "I know that this is hard, Mrs. Wilson."

A sad smile played on the woman's lips as she blinked back tears.

"Do you, now? Have you spent the last nine years praying, holding your breath, waiting for your daughter to come home?"

"No, ma'am," Suzie replied quietly and with contrition.

The next moment, the woman collected herself. "I'm sorry, I don't mean to sound bitter. You're only trying to help and I appreciate that." She looked from one of them to the other. Disengaging her hands from Suzie's, she rose to her feet again. "I have a hairbrush. Will that help?"

"A hairbrush will be perfect," Suzie told her.

"I'll be right back," Amy promised, leaving the room.

She was back in moments, handing Suzie an expensive looking hairbrush, the kind that might be part of a three-piece set.

"Her father gave her that," Mrs. Wilson said after a moment's hesitation. "We divorced three years after Cara went missing. He blamed me for being too permissive. I don't know, maybe he was right..." she murmured, her eyes filling with tears again.

She wiped them away angrily.

"It's not your fault, Mrs. Wilson," Chris told her gently. "Girls that age are going to do whatever they want to do, whatever they think is right. I've got three sisters, I know," he explained in an understanding voice. He indicated the hairbrush in Suzie's hand. "We'll bring this back as soon as we can."

"And you'll tell me?" Amy asked, walking them to the front door. "If the girl you found is Cara, you will tell me?"

"We'll tell you," he promised.

"Thank you," she whispered, as she closed the door.

Twilight had descended as he and Suzie were talking with Cara's mother. "Are you all right?" Chris finally asked, when Suzie made no effort to say anything as they drove back to Aurora in the dark.

Seeing Mrs. Wilson only reminded her of all the mothers whose daughters her father had killed. It had taken her a few minutes to get her anger back under control.

"I'm not the one waiting to find out if her daughter is lying in some unmarked grave," she told him, still struggling with her anger.

"Cremated," he corrected quietly.

What he said wasn't registering. "What?"

"Bodies that aren't claimed or identified after thirty days are cremated," he reminded her.

For some reason, that had just slipped her mind. "So Mrs. Wilson really won't have closure," she whispered in a stilted voice.

"She still will, of a sort," Chris qualified. "If the hairs on the brush turn out to match the DNA they had on file."

Suzie supposed he had a point, in a manner of speaking, but it still wasn't the kind of peace the woman would have wanted.

"You were very understanding back there," Suzie said, after a few more minutes had passed. "With Mrs. Wilson," she added, in case he missed what she was trying to say.

He only wished he could have done more for the woman, comforted her somehow.

"It's not easy, hearing that someone you love is never coming home again. There is no good way to break the news."

"No, there isn't," Suzie agreed. "Still, you were very kind."

He laughed softly. "You say that as if you're surprised."

She was going to deny it, or say something flippant in response, then reconsidered. He'd impressed her with the way he'd been with Mrs. Wilson, and she felt as if she should somehow acknowledge the fact. At the very least, she owed him the truth.

"Maybe I am, a little," she allowed.

She was being nice. Chris changed the subject, thinking that he should quit while he was ahead.

"We'll log that brush into Evidence for the night and then see about getting testing okayed in the morning."

"It's better to ask for forgiveness than permission," she told him.

"In this case, given who your boss is, it might be smarter to do it the other way around," Chris suggested. Suzie began to protest, but he cut her off, saying, "Uncle Sean isn't a stickler and he doesn't envision himself being a dictator over a small realm. As a matter of fact, he's pretty damn easygoing. But he might take it personally if he finds that you've gone rogue—and there's no way you can verify if that dead girl is Cara Wilson without either getting his permission to run the test, or going rogue and doing it. The latter course might cost you more than you realize. Not to mention that using it as evidence for some reason down the line would be totally out of the question if you decide to go that route."

Suzie sighed. He was right. She couldn't really argue with anything he'd said.

"You have a point."

One hand on the wheel, he pretended to clutch at his chest with his other one. When she looked at him, not knowing if she should be concerned, he said, "Thankfully, I have a strong heart. Otherwise, you'd be rushing me to the hospital right about now."

The more time she spent with this man, the less she understood him, Suzie thought. "What the hell are you talking about?"

"I almost had a heart attack."

She struggled to keep from saying a few choice things. Instead, she stated, "All right, I'll bite. Why did you almost have a heart attack?"

Sparing her a quick look, he allowed his mouth to curve. "Because you just gave me an out-and-out compliment."

"Well, that'll certainly teach me a lesson," Suzie said drily. "Trust me, it won't happen again."

He merely laughed in response, as if he knew something she didn't.

Suzie hardly got any sleep all night.

Thinking about the DNA test she wanted to run, anticipating its outcome, she could hardly wait to get started. Consequently, she was dressed and ready hours before she knew she could actually go in.

But when she finally did arrive at the lab, she knew that Chris had been right. She had to go through the proper steps to do the test, or she couldn't legally do it at all.

Though she had tried hard to pace herself, she'd wound up getting to the lab ahead of Sean. However, true to his nature, the manager of the lab's day shift wasn't that far behind her.

She was waiting for him in his office.

"Should I be concerned?" he asked, putting his container of coffee on his desk. Sitting down, he removed the lid, but didn't take a sip.

"Why?"

"Well, I'm used to your being in the lab ahead of me. I've come to expect it, actually. The last couple of weeks, with you being up in Homicide, it felt almost strange walking in and not seeing you here. But finding you in my office is another story." Sean felt there had to be a reason the young woman was waiting for him. "You're either here to tell me about a breakthrough, or that you're leaving."

"Leaving?" she echoed. Why would he think she was leaving? She was happier here, working with these people, than she'd been for a long time. She was just beginning to feel as if she actually belonged somewhere. "Why would you think that I was leaving?"

"I thought it might have something to do with Chris," he said honestly. "He's a really good detective and a great nephew, but he's also probably not what you're used to. For some, Chris is an acquired taste. I thought maybe you and he had come to some kind of an impasse and you'd decided to leave the department rather than having to put up with him anymore."

Stunned, Suzie could only shake her head. "No, none of the above."

"All right," Sean said, pausing to take a long sip of his coffee. He got comfortable in his chair. "So why are you here, brightening up my office?"

She knew he was being kind. She hadn't brightened up any place she'd been in the last three years. "I came to ask for your permission."

She had definitely piqued his interest. Polite, sharp, an above-average hard worker, Suzie Quinn still wasn't the type who came right out and asked for permission—for anything.

"To do what?" he asked.

Damn O'Bannon; he'd made her nervous about this. "I want to run a DNA test."

Sean waited, expecting her to say more. He didn't understand. Suzie didn't need permission for that. It went without saying that she could run the test. It was what was done here.

No, this had to be about something different, he decided.

"Help me out here," Sean requested. "What makes this DNA test so unusual that you feel you have to ask for special permission?"

Suzie was tempted to quit while she was ahead.

But that would be dishonest and she wouldn't lie to him, even by omission. Her boss needed to know the details.

"The DNA belongs to a girl who's been dead for nine years."

He did a quick mental review of the cases he knew were currently opened. "I wasn't aware that we had a cold case involving a dead girl."

"It's not one of ours. The body was found in Oak Valley."

She paused, holding her breath and waiting for her boss to tell her that their budget was already stretched to the limit doing tests on the bodies within Aurora's jurisdiction. But he didn't.

"Go on, I'm listening."

When she spoke again, she found herself talking rapidly, trying to get everything in before he decided to cut her off.

"Since we have the technology available now, I thought that maybe we could ID her and bring her mother some peace."

Sean appeared mildly surprised. "Then you know her mother?"

"Well, I met her yesterday."

He liked the fact that Suzie didn't lie or twist the facts to suit her purposes. "And you have something with this girl's DNA?"

"Yes. Her mother gave us a hairbrush. It's bagged in Evidence at the moment."

Nodding, Sean was quiet for a moment, as if he was thinking something over. And then he said, "Tell you what, I'll let you run the test if you do something for me."

He was the father that she wished she'd actually had. Truthful, forthright, honest. Generous to a fault and always willing to help anyone who came to him. Suzie was willing to do anything for the man and wasn't ashamed of saying so.

"Of course, sir, anything."

"My brother's having this get-together this Saturday…" Sean began.

Her eyes widened. She knew exactly where this was going. What she didn't understand was why. "Why is it so important to you people that I attend?" she demanded.

"Well, you know, the more the merrier—"

"From what I've heard, sir, if there were any more there, the place would have to be zoned as a small city."

He laughed. "That's just a testimony to how many people enjoy attending my brother's little get-togethers. So, what do you say? Will you come?"

Chris had put him up to this, she was sure of it. But she was also certain that Sean was serious. At bottom, she told herself, this was a trade of favors. She had to think of it as such.

"All right, sir, I'll come—as long as I can run the test."

Sean nodded. "You can run the test, Suzie."

Doing her best not to look uncomfortable, she nodded back. "Thank you, sir. And yes, I'll come to the chief of police's party."

Sean's smile was wide and all encompassing. A little like his nephew's.

"*Former* chief of police," he corrected. "And you won't regret agreeing to come, Suzie."

That was his opinion and he had a right to it, but as for her, she was already regretting saying yes. Because now she had to go. A person had to be as good as their word, or else what was the point?

Chapter 13

"You chew on that lip any harder and there's going to be a gaping hole in it."

Suzie hadn't expected anyone to come up to her while she was working in the lab. The other CSIs who comprised her usual team were out, investigating the scene of a home invasion. Sean had left for a meeting, so she had naturally assumed that she was alone in the lab.

Obviously, she wasn't.

Trying not to look as startled as she felt, Suzie glanced up. By then, the man who had invaded her space—as well as her unguarded dreams—had already crossed the room and was now in front of her, almost larger than life. Which was the way she usually thought of Chris O'Bannon, though she would have never admitted as much to him.

"What are you doing down here?" she asked.

Unfazed, he said, "I was going to ask you the same thing."

She went back to what she was doing, preparing the DNA sample so it could be matched against the hairs on the brush that Mrs. Wilson had lent her. "I am working," she said in a measured voice.

"Which was what you've been doing lately upstairs," he told her patiently. "Have you decided to give up?"

The expression in her eyes when she raised them to his answered his question. In no uncertain terms.

"No, of course not. You're a pit bull. You latch on to something and you don't let go."

She gave him a withering look and got back to what she was doing. "If you don't mind a little constructive criticism, O'Bannon, I think you need to brush up a bit on your flattery skills."

"I'm not trying to flatter you, Suzie Q," he told her. "I'm just making an observation. And for the record, I think pit bulls have gotten a bum rap and have been pretty maligned. Trained correctly, they can be very loving, sweet pets."

She didn't care for the veiled message she thought the detective was conveying. "I'm not about to allow anyone to try to 'train' me, O'Bannon."

The very idea of someone attempting to get the feisty investigator to do anything made him laugh. "I sincerely doubt anyone could ever even try," he retorted. "Now, if you haven't given up on the case, and you obviously haven't, just what are you doing back down here in the lab?"

She had always hated being questioned by someone who had no right to do so. O'Bannon had no authority over her and he wasn't her superior, no matter what he thought of himself or what he believed his family connections bought him.

Grudgingly, she told him, "I got permission to run the DNA sample to see if it matches up to the Wilson girl."

"Permission," Chris repeated. And then he smiled, pleased. "So you took my advice."

She knew he was going to take credit for this. She was surprised he wasn't dislocating his shoulder, patting himself on the back.

"Let's just say I went the logical route," she told him tersely.

The smile turned into a grin. A wide one. "Kills you to say it, doesn't it?"

She spared him one annoyed glance. "I don't know what you mean."

"So does this mean you'll be tied up down here all day? Reason I'm asking is because I'm going back in the field and just thought you might want to come along."

Her eyes narrowed at his wording. "You make me sound like some puppy you expect to just come running after you."

Even in a lab coat, with her hair pulled back, making her appear like an old-fashioned schoolmarm, the woman still looked hot. She just seemed totally unaware of it, which made her even hotter, in his opinion.

"No one would ever mistake you for a puppy, Suzie Q. Trust me," Chris assured her. He began to edge away. "I'll let you know how it goes."

Suzie knew she should just ignore him. But she couldn't. Her curiosity had gotten the better of her. "Who are you going to question?"

"I thought since we weren't getting anywhere talking to any of the people who were at that party," he said casually, playing out his line like a fishing pro, "maybe we should be talking to the people we know were supposedly *behind* the party."

She was instantly alert. "You mean Warren Eldridge?"

"And Simon Silas," he reminded her, still retreating from her toward the doorway. "There might be more, but for now, we have those two names."

Suzie made up her mind. The DNA test would take two days whether she was here or not. She might as well be productive while she waited.

"Wait," she cried, shedding the lab coat the same way a snake sheds its skin. She tossed it onto a chair. "I'm coming with you, O'Bannon," she called after him.

Hurrying to catch up, Suzie pulled off the rubber band holding back her hair and ran her hand through her locks, trying to coax them into order.

Chris paused by the doorway, waiting. "Knew you couldn't resist me."

"It's not you," she informed him. "I want to be there when you talk to those two, just in case you get tongue-tied or mesmerized by the fact that when they walk, hundred-dollar bills fall in their wake."

Chris pressed for the elevator. "Money doesn't impress me, Suzie Q. Hard work and dedication, those are my downfall."

"Yeah, that and a size two with a tight butt." She'd meant to only think that, not have it come out of her mouth.

"You're a size two?" he asked. She couldn't tell if he was surprised or just teasing her. In either case, she wasn't about to pursue the conversation. Some things were meant to be left in the dark on the closet floor.

"Never mind what my size is. I'll drive," she told him as they got into the elevator.

"Not a chance." They were on the first floor in the blink of an eye.

"Why not?" she asked. She exited the elevator first, but he had a longer stride and reached the rear door before her. "You drove all the other times."

"And I got used to it," he answered pleasantly, holding it open for her. She glared at him as she marched out. "As to why not, let's just say I want to go on living."

She hurried down the steps to the lot. "What's that supposed to mean?"

"It means I've seen you pulling up into the parking lot," he told her, then added a shiver for effect to make his point.

"When?" she demanded.

"A few weeks ago." Spotting his vehicle, he made his way to it. Suzie was forced to follow. "I was the car you almost ran down."

That rang no bells. "I don't remember almost running down a car."

"I know," he said. He pressed on the key chain and all four locks popped up. "Point made."

Several retorts were burning on her tongue, but she bit them back. There was an outside chance that he was right. She did have a tendency to get distracted when she was lost in thought, and just because she hadn't noticed a near run-in with another car didn't mean that there hadn't almost been one.

Throwing open the door on her side, she grudgingly got in.

"Where are we going first?" she asked the detective some ten minutes later.

"Ah, she speaks."

"Cut the sarcasm or you'll *really* hear me speak," she warned him.

"Fair enough," he allowed. "I figure we'll start at the top."

"Doesn't answer my question." There were two men seen on that video who could occupy that lofty position.

"Well, although two men attending this not-so-secret bash are what the rest of us call 'obscenely' wealthy, Warren Eldridge's got more than a slight edge in this department."

"So we're going to see Warren Eldridge?" she asked.

"There's that keen mind again," Chris acknowledged.

She wanted to wipe that smile off his face, but a part of her wasn't thinking about using her fist to do it—which irritated her even more.

Warren Eldridge, the CEO of one of the country's leading tech companies, seemed to have a slight edge in every department. Young, good-looking, with both sailing and tennis skills that made him the envy of award-winning champions in those fields, he was sought after for speaking engagements as well as personal engagements, many of the latter by women who were eager for a chance to land the exceptionally eligible bachelor.

Warren Eldridge's office was on the top floor of the building that bore his name. Although he had called ahead to make sure the man was on the premises, Chris still had to explain to an administrative assistant why they were there.

After listening in stony silence, the humorless-looking staffer, a tall, lean, perfectly manicured young man who'd introduced himself as Lionel, said, "Yes, Mr. Eldridge said he was expecting you.

"You're in luck," Lionel told them as he led the way down a long hallway. "Most of the time, Mr. Eldridge is in transit, traveling between cities or states. Even his GPS can't keep up with him," he added drily.

"I've never seen so many testimonials, awards and photographs," Suzie whispered to Chris under her breath, scanning the walls on either side of the hall as they were led to Eldridge's penultimate office. "Is he trying to impress people?"

"My guess is *intimidate*," Chris whispered back. Seeing Eldridge with world leaders and the heads of well-regarded charitable foundations was enough to cause a lot of people he knew to become speechless.

That went double for the handful of framed photographs of a younger-looking Eldridge standing next to a statuesque blonde who looked too gorgeous for words.

In total, the photographs—especially the ones with the blonde—were enough to make them back away from wanting to question the man about anything that might have to do with a young woman's murder.

Suzie tended to agree with Chris's assessment. "So you're not just a pretty face," she cracked.

"Oh, I'm that, too," he assured her so seriously that for a second she thought he was being serious.

But there was just the faintest glimmer in his eyes that told her to think again.

Warren Eldridge turned out to be even better looking in person than he was in his pictures, and just a little larger than life. When they entered, he turned around from his computer, flashing a smile that exhibited teeth, whitened to perfection.

Ending a conversation on his cell phone, he

pocketed it and rose from his desk, then crossed his office to meet them.

An office, Suzie couldn't help thinking, that could have housed all the people in the new homeless shelter he'd just dedicated last month to the memory of his late mother.

The man was either very close to sainthood or he'd come from central casting to fill that role. Suzie wasn't sure which description she felt was more likely.

"It's not every day that I have law enforcement agents coming to my office to see me." Eldridge smiled warmly at them, his expressive blue eyes moving from one to the other.

For a moment, Suzie felt as if those eyes were lingering on her cross, and she resisted the temptation to cover it with her hand. The next second Eldridge turned his attention to O'Bannon.

"What is it that I can do for you, Detectives?"

Chris got the introductions out of the way, although he had a feeling that Eldridge already knew their names. Warren Eldridge hadn't gotten to where he was by not doing his homework and doing it diligently.

"I'm Detective Christian O'Bannon and this is CSI Susannah Quinn."

Shaking their hands, the philanthropist CEO looked at Suzie intently, as if he was trying to place her. His hand still around hers, he addressed his words to Chris. "I think you mean Susannah Quinlan, don't you, Detective?"

Suzie felt as if an ice pick had pierced her, but she kept her expression stony. “No, it’s Quinn, Mr. Eldridge,” she told the man firmly.

Eldridge inclined his head. “My mistake. For a moment, you reminded me of someone I thought I’d seen somewhere else. The mind plays tricks sometimes,” he confessed. His eyes shifting back to Chris, he asked, “So, why are you here? Some worthwhile cause you’d like me to contribute to?”

“No,” Chris answered. “We’re just here for some information. We’d like to ask you about a party you threw a week ago last Sunday.”

Eldridge sighed, looking like a man accustomed to being at the center of rumors and misinformation. “I’m afraid someone gave you a bad piece of intel, Detective. I didn’t throw any party last week, or the week before that,” he added for good measure.

Suzie began giving the CEO clues to jar his memory. “The abandoned department store, Kresky’s. A couple of boys tried to crash the bash, but according to them, they were turned away. But they still managed to take a few videos through one of the windows that hadn’t been blacked out.”

“We have a few good likenesses of you,” Chris added, taking blown-up stills of Eldridge that had been made from the videos. He spread them out one by one on the desk.

Not a single muscle of Eldridge’s face twitched. The man was good. “A lot of people look like me, Detective.”

Chris left the photographs where they were. "So you were never there?"

Eldridge never blinked. He did, however, smile, pouring on the charm that had likely been a major asset in building his empire. "I didn't say that."

"What did you say?" Suzie asked.

He was all too willing to explain. "That I didn't throw the party, as you suggested. I did help fund it, as did a few other acquaintances of mine. But I wouldn't call that 'throwing a party.' That's far too plebian a term, don't you think?"

What she was thinking right now, Suzie reflected, could land her in jail. But it might be worth it, if it meant wiping that look off the man's face. Whether he was guilty or not, she didn't like Eldridge or his manner. There was just something about him that got under her skin.

"Did you happen to see this young woman there?" Chris asked, removing Eldridge's photographs and replacing them with two of Bethany, taken from different angles.

Eldridge assessed both pictures. "Is it just me, or does this young woman have no clothes on?" he asked, looking up at Chris.

The detective's eyes darkened. "It's not you," he answered. "She doesn't."

Eldridge laughed drily and Suzie found she had to struggle to restrain herself. The man might very well be innocent of Bethany's murder, but he was guilty of being an ass and a first-class jerk.

"I assure you, Detective," he was saying, "I would

have remembered seeing a woman with no clothes on—and I didn't," he concluded simply.

"She's also dead," Suzie pointed out, rather needlessly, she thought, given Bethany's lack of color.

Eldridge merely shook his head, as if her addition just backed up his version. "I didn't see a dead woman at the party, either."

"Look again," Chris requested. "Someone estimated that there were almost a thousand people attending that party."

Hearing the number only seemed to please Eldridge, as if it was another testimonial to add to his list. "Go big or go home—isn't that the popular phrase these days, Detective?"

"I'm not up on popular phrases," Chris replied, his eyes on Eldridge's. "I'm too busy trying to solve murders."

"I really wish I could help, Detective, I do," the man said with sincerity. "But I'm afraid I can't. I was only there for a brief period, just to make sure that everything was going well. Too crowded for my tastes, really," he confided.

"Where did you go after you left the bash?" Chris asked him.

"I had another party to go to," Eldridge said, as casually as if this was something they should have known. "I work very, very hard most of the time, Detective O'Bannon. But even a smart phone needs to recharge once in a while. This—" he indicated the pile of photographs of him that Chris had put to the side "—is how I recharge."

"Can anyone vouch for your being at the other party?" Suzie challenged.

"Absolutely." There was enthusiasm in Eldridge's voice. "I can give you a list—a who's who list of the richest people in the state," he told them matter-of-factly, saying it as if that should bring an end to any further question.

Picking up a pad from his desk, he dashed off the names, including the governor, two past senators and the winner of last year's academy award, then tore the paper from the pad and handed it not to Chris but to Suzie.

"By the way, if you ever decide that you'd like a little change of pace from catching 'bad guys,' just give me a call, Ms. Quinlan."

"Quinn," she corrected between clenched teeth.

He'd done that on purpose, she thought. The question was why? Did he recognize her from the clips that had been in the paper or on the internet? But that had been three years ago. She'd moved, gotten a degree under her new name. There was no reason for Eldridge to have made the mistake.

Unless it wasn't a mistake on his part.

"Sorry, my mistake again." The apology dripped of graciousness. He handed her a card. "My personal number's on the back. Now, if there's nothing else, I'm afraid I have a meeting I need to get to. I promised to chair a fund-raiser for the children's hospital in San Francisco. Tugs on your heart, seeing those kids going through pain like that. I've just got to try to do something about it, nudge other people to do something, too." He glanced from the detective to the woman with him. "I can give you the details if either one of you are free."

"We'll get back to you on that," Chris told him.

"All right, then, I'll be waiting for your call, Detective. Until then, Lionel here will escort you back to the elevator. This building's a positive maze and I wouldn't want you getting lost."

Within a moment, the administrative assistant came for them, practically materializing out of nowhere.

"We can find the elevators on our own," Chris assured the stately, well-dressed assistant.

"Mr. Eldridge would prefer if I escorted you," Lionel told them without any inflection in his voice.

"Think he rusts in the rain?" Chris asked once they were in the elevator.

"I don't know, but I do know that I want to take a shower as soon as I get back to the precinct." When Chris gave her a questioning look, she said, "Eldridge gives me the absolute creeps. There's something almost slimy about him."

"From those photographs on his wall," Chris pointed out, "a lot of people would disagree with you."

"A lot of people just want a piece of his pie," Suzie countered.

Chris nodded. "Probably truer than you think."

"Hey, O'Bannon, did you happen to notice that one photograph of him on the tennis court?"

He thought for a moment, then recalled the photograph she was referring to. "What about it?"

"He was holding his racket in his left hand."

"Which means he's left-handed," Chris realized.

"Which means he's left-handed," Suzie concluded, with what Chris could have sworn was a smile of vindication.

Chapter 14

"We're going to need more than that if we want to be able to charge Eldridge with the murder," Chris pointed out. "Right now, his being left-handed just comes under the heading of 'circumstantial.'"

Did he think she didn't know that? "Of course we need more," she retorted. "I was just pointing out the obvious," she added defensively.

He got into the car, then waited until she followed suit and closed her door.

"What was that back there?" he asked.

She *knew* O'Bannon wasn't going to let the billionaire's remark go. Crossing her fingers, she pretended not to know what he was referring to. Maybe he'd just drop it. "You mean other than him being a preening peacock?"

She was dodging his question, which made him even more suspicious. "I mean the bit with Eldridge thinking your last name was Quinlan."

She shrugged, continuing to look out of the front window. "He obviously made a mistake."

Chris would have agreed with her, except for one thing. "Is that why you looked so pale when he mentioned that other name?"

"I wasn't pale." Realizing that she was raising her voice, Suzie deliberately lowered it before continuing. "I just found him pushy and annoying."

He thought of all the people who were eagerly trying to secure just five minutes of the man's time. The photographs on his wall bore testimony to that. "You'd be in the minority."

Unfazed, Suzie shrugged her shoulders. "Doesn't mean I'm wrong."

"No," he agreed, "it doesn't." Pausing at a red light, he looked thoughtfully at the woman beside him and changed the subject. "You feel up to interviewing Simon Silas with me, or would you rather I took you back to the lab so you could babysit that DNA test?"

They both knew the test wouldn't go any faster if she was hovering over it, waiting for results. He'd be the first to point that out. Was he trying to get rid of her?

"I'm fine, O'Bannon. Just drive," she ordered, "and let's go see what Silas has to say."

* * *

What Simon Silas had to say consisted of two words: "Go away."

The much sought after movie producer, mogul and would-be philanthropist was on his way out when they were shown into his office by one of the three receptionists Silas kept out front.

The producer's office suite was smaller than Eldridge's, but far more ostentatious in its decor. His walls had just as many, if not more, framed photographs of the man, taken with a whole host of celebrities, both current and past. He was photographed with a lot more attractive women than Eldridge had been, as well.

Another difference between the two was that Silas was not nearly as genial and charming as Eldridge had been at their meeting. In fact, he was waspish and curt.

His mood did not change when he saw their credentials. Instead, he continued to make his way out of the office and to the elevator.

"Talk to my assistant. The one that looks like she knows something," he told Chris.

Chris deliberately placed himself in the man's way. They were both the same height, and for a moment, it appeared to be a stalemate.

Silas scowled. "You caught me at a bad time, Officer," he snapped, attempting to circumvent the situation.

"That's Detective," Chris corrected.

The next moment, Suzie blocked the man's path, preventing him from going anywhere.

"When would be a good time?" Suzie challenged.

"I've got a few hours free at the end of November," Silas answered coldly. "Why don't you check back with me then?"

"Sorry, not good enough," Chris told him. Through with playing games, he told the movie producer, "We'll settle for a few minutes now—either here or at the precinct. This is a murder investigation." There was no arguing with his tone.

Silas sighed. "All right. Civic duty and all that," he muttered. But rather than head back to his office, he instructed, "Walk with me to my car."

With that he continued to make his way to the elevator.

Settling for the flimsy compromise, Chris decided to accompany the movie producer to the elevator, and ultimately, to his car. He could always still take the man in if Silas's answers weren't satisfactory.

Reaching the end of the hallway, Silas pressed for the elevator. It arrived almost immediately. Once on it, he turned and looked at Suzie, on his right.

"Anyone ever tell you that you have fantastic cheekbones? Ever consider a career in movies?" he asked. It was obvious by his manner that the line had served him well in the past.

Suzie narrowed her eyes, summarily rejecting what the producer was prepared to suggest. "I prefer forensics," she informed him.

Reaching over, Chris halted the elevator in mid-descent.

Startled, Silas demanded, “What the hell are you doing?”

“Getting your attention. Mr. Silas.” Chris calmly took the photograph of Bethany out of the folder he was carrying and held it up.

“Get that out of my face,” the movie producer snapped, waving it away. “What is it, a still from some cheap horror movie?”

“No,” Chris said, setting the man straight, “that’s a photograph of a woman who might have attended that so-called secret bash that you and your friend Warren Eldridge, underwrote and attended in the abandoned department store.”

Silas’s deeply tanned complexion darkened even more. “Just what are you accusing me of?” he demanded hotly.

“Nothing yet,” Chris answered mildly. “Right now, all I want to know is if you recognize her.” He held the photograph up again.

Silas pushed it away a second time. “No!” Appearing more than a little agitated, the man demanded, “Now can I go?”

“For now,” Chris allowed. Reaching over again, he pressed the button to restart the elevator. “We’ll get back to you.”

“There’s no point,” Silas insisted. “I never saw that woman—alive or dead. I was with friends,” he told Chris haughtily, then cited five names, all of which belonged to well-known actresses. “Call them," he snapped. "I'll even give you their phone numbers."

"That would be helpful," Chris agreed, in a docile manner that further irritated the producer.

By now they had reached the ground floor. Taking out his worn notebook, Chris handed it to the producer. Carrying it was something he had picked up from one of his cousins, who believed in jotting down notes while they were still fresh in his mind rather than dictating them into an app on his smart phone.

Biting off a few choice words, Silas quickly wrote down the names and cell phone numbers of all five actresses, then pushed the notebook back in annoyance.

"So, are we done?" he asked.

"For now," Chris repeated.

The producer stormed off to his vehicle, cursing a blue streak as he went.

"Notice anything?" Chris asked Suzie as he pocketed the notebook.

"Yes." She knew exactly what he was referring to. She'd watched as the producer had written down the names of the women he was using as his alibis. "Silas is left-handed, too."

"Hell of a coincidence," Chris remarked. "If it were strictly up to me, of the two I'd pick him for the doer. Although I'd have to admit it is kind of stereotypical."

"There's a reason for stereotypical," Suzie told

him as they got back into his car. "A lot of it is based on a layer of fact."

Intrigued, Chris paused before starting his engine. "So you think Silas killed Bethany?"

Something in her gut had told her it was Eldridge, but then, after being around Silas, she found herself thinking it might be him. She needed more.

"I don't know yet," she admitted.

"Indecision," Chris noted with an approving nod. "It's a start." With that, he started up the vehicle. "So, about tomorrow."

There was just no such thing as relaxing around this man, she thought irritably. "What about tomorrow?"

Guiding the car out of the parking structure, he said, "It's Saturday."

"Usually comes after Friday," Suzie responded, doing her best to keep the conversation as vague as humanly possible.

He ignored what he took to be sarcasm and became more specific. "I hear that Uncle Sean got you to agree to come to the get-together."

"'Agree' makes it sound as if it was voluntary on my part," she pointed out, and it was no such thing. "He bribed me."

Chris saw nothing wrong with that. "Hey, whatever gets you to the gathering..." He deliberately let his voice trail off.

"Gathering," she echoed. "You make it sound like some kind of a benign counsel meeting."

He was not about to get sucked into a war of

words. "Nobody counseling anybody, just a lot of stories being swapped while eating some *really* good food," he told her with enthusiasm.

From what she'd heard, these things occurred all the time. The Cavanaughs at the precinct worked alongside family members all week. Why would they want to get together in their off-hours?

"Is this mandatory for you people?" she asked.

"If you're asking does everyone come to every one of these things, the answer's no. If you're asking do we *want* to come to every one of Uncle Andrew's get-togethers, then the answer's yes. But is attending the get-togethers 'mandatory'? No, of course not." He sighed as he turned down another major street. "Why, are you trying to find a way to wiggle out of it?"

"No!" Suzie all but snapped out her denial in no uncertain terms. She didn't like him trying to get inside her head.

Chris was about to say something in response when his cell phone rang. He frowned, hoping it wasn't something bad. Holding on to the steering wheel with one hand, he pulled his phone from his pocket with the other and swiped it with his thumb.

"O'Bannon," he declared as he held the device near his ear.

Wondering if it was a private call, Suzie glanced at his face as he listened to whoever was on the other end.

His expression told her this was business, not

pleasure—not that it mattered to her, she silently insisted.

"Right," he said grimly. "I know where that is. On our way." Terminating the call, Chris sighed as he dropped the phone back in his pocket.

Suzie didn't like the grim set of his jaw. "You know where what is?" she asked.

"The location of the body," he told her, making an abrupt U-turn.

"What body?" she asked, even though she had a sinking feeling in the pit of her stomach that she already knew the answer to that.

His answer was short and to the point. "Our killer struck again."

She thought of the list of victims they had put together, all blondes, all in their midtwenties, who were very possibly connected to the man who had killed Bethany Miller. And now O'Bannon was telling her there was another one?

"Just now?" she questioned.

"Won't know that until the ME makes his—or her—call," Chris told her. He flipped on the siren as he sped up.

When was this going to end? Suzie wondered, feeling sick to her stomach. "Why do they think it's the same killer?"

He cited the description he'd just been given. "Twentysomething semi-nude blonde, strangled. Sound familiar?"

Her mouth had gone dry. "Too familiar," she answered.

* * *

The latest victim had been found in a recently abandoned movie theater by a homeless man who'd gone in seeking shelter. The old theater, once a majestic opera house, had just been sold and was about to be renovated and turned into a multiplex.

"Let me guess—this was the scene of another party?" Suzie asked Sean when they arrived.

Her boss had gotten there ahead of them with the rest of his team and had just begun to investigate the crime scene.

Sean lowered the high-definition camera he was using to capture details of the scene and shook his head. He couldn't say one way or another.

"If it was, I want to hire whoever cleaned this place up after the party, because there isn't anything left to indicate there ever *was* a party thrown here. That doesn't mean that there wasn't," he was quick to qualify. "Jury's still out on that."

The victim was almost out of sight, hidden against what had been a concession stand. Chris crossed over to the young woman. She could have been Bethany Miller's twin. There was no question about it, the killer definitely had a type.

"Same bruising on the left side?" Chris asked his uncle.

Sean nodded. "Looks that way. Oh, and there's one more piece to add to the puzzle," he said, just as Chris began to turn away.

"Go ahead," Chris urged.

"The killer's tall," Sean told them.

"Because he picks tall blondes?" Suzie asked, guessing at how Sean had come to that conclusion.

But her boss shook his head. "No. A lot of short men like tall women. All of Mickey Rooney's wives were taller than he was," he cited.

Suzie exchanged looks with Chris. She saw that he didn't recognize the name, either. "Who?"

"Never mind," Sean answered. "I'm showing my age. The point I'm getting at is that the killer didn't just strangle his victims, he lifted them off the ground while he was doing it. In order to do that, he had to be taller than they were."

"Okay," Suzie replied. "Left-handed and tall, not to mention strong. It takes a certain kind of strength to be able to lift them off the ground like that." She tried not to dwell on the image. "Looks like we're narrowing the cesspool," she commented.

"In the meantime," Chris said, "we need to find out who bought this property."

"You think it was Eldridge?" she asked.

But Chris gave no indication one way or another. "All I'm thinking is that we needed to get every scrap of information we can to build this case. Eventually, it'll lead us to the bastard who's killing these women."

Eventually.

The word seemed to echo in her head.

"You really believe that?" she asked as they left the premises.

"I have to," Chris answered. "Otherwise, I wouldn't be able to do my job. Hell, I wouldn't be able to get up in the morning. Speaking of morning," he said as they finally got back to his car, "what time do you want me to pick you up tomorrow?"

Preoccupied with this latest murder, Suzie stared at him. It took her a couple seconds to connect the dots. When she finally did, she said, "I don't."

"You want to drive to Uncle Andrew's in your car?" he questioned. "You know where his house is?"

He made it sound as if the former chief of police's house was located in some mysterious hidden valley. "I'll find it," she answered.

The way she put it, Chris came to the only logical conclusion he could. "So you *don't* know where his house is."

She wasn't sure whether or not to be insulted. She supposed O'Bannon meant well. But she didn't like being perceived as a hapless female. That was the *last* thing she was.

"I've been finding places in this city for the last two years," she informed him. "Don't worry, I'll find his."

"Yeah, but that means you'll have to park your car."

"Well, I don't plan on carrying it in with me." Just what was he getting at?

"What I mean is that if everyone comes to the gathering in their own car, that's going to be a hell of a lot of cars out there, taking up an awful lot of space. It's a lot smarter if we carpooled."

Before she could make a comment on that one

way or another, he told her, "I'll pick you up at eleven—unless you want to go earlier."

"No." What she wanted was to not go at all, but she knew that wouldn't fly. These Cavanaughs seemed to get their way no matter what the objections. She tried one last argument. "But if we go together, we have to leave together."

Chris nodded. "Sounds right."

Did she have to hit him over the head with a two-by-four? "What I'm trying to say is that I might want to leave before you do."

And then he said what she was afraid he was going to say, totally invalidating her last defense against going with him. "I promise to leave whenever you're ready to go, no questions asked."

Yeah, right. She didn't buy it for a second. "How gullible do you think I am?" she asked.

"I don't think you're gullible at all, Suzie Q," he told her. "Scout's honor," he declared. "You say the word and we're gone."

There was no way she could envision him being a Boy Scout. Not with that glint in his eyes. "When were you a Scout?" she asked.

He was ready for her. "You want to call my mother and ask? She has pictures to prove it," he told her.

She didn't know if she believed him or not, but she did know that the Cavanaughs had a tendency to stick together and back one another up, so there was no point in even pretending she was going to ask for proof.

She was going to this thing and there was no getting out of it.

"No," Suzie answered with a sigh. "I'll take your word for it."

"Face it, Suzie Q," he told her as he drove back to the precinct's parking lot. "You and I really need this break. The case is getting hot and we need to step back for a second in order to maintain the proper perspective on it."

Arguing wasn't going to get her anywhere. Besides, there was a part of her that tended to agree with him. "Maybe you're right," she conceded.

"I usually am."

Then again, his answer made her contemplate strangling him, which, all things considered, seemed rather appropriate in this case.

"I wouldn't go that far," she murmured under her breath.

Chris heard her, but pretended not to. He just smiled to himself.

Chapter 15

How bad could it be?

The question she'd asked herself echoed over and over in Suzie's head as she went through the motions of getting ready for the Cavanaugh gathering she'd said she would attend.

Ordinarily, preparing to leave the house was an automatic ritual, but for the last three years, all she'd gotten ready for was to go to work. Here, and before Aurora, for in the crime lab where she'd worked in Phoenix.

All that getting ready required of her was to shower, then get dressed in something that was serviceable and allowed her to hit the ground running when a crime scene was involved.

In these last three years, she hadn't once "gone

out" in the normal definition of the term. She hadn't seen anyone socially, either alone or in a group, except for that one failed attempt when Chris had tried to pick her up. With a sigh, Suzie realized that she was all but a hermit now, and mingling was beyond her usual scope of life. She didn't mingle, didn't socialize and didn't do well in crowds, all of which she knew this afternoon definitely promised.

She shouldn't have agreed, she told herself as she stared, unseeing, at her wardrobe mirror.

She needed to "unagree" the moment O'Bannon came to her door, to pick her up as if she were a package to be delivered.

What was the worst thing that would happen? Chris would leave without her, possibly mumbling something less than flattering about her under his breath. Nothing she hadn't been subjected to before. No matter how annoyed he might get by her reversal, he certainly wasn't going to grab her by her hair and drag her to this thing like some lumbering caveman.

"All you have to do is say no. You know how to say no, don't you?" she challenged the woman looking back at her in the mirror. "You've heard the word often enough," she murmured, remembering her other life after the roof had caved in.

Suzie squared her shoulders and psyched herself up, ready to launch into the fray—until she heard the doorbell.

Suddenly, her shoulders seemed to cave in as the sound registered.

He was here.

"Hang tough," she ordered her reflection. The girl in the light blue sundress looked uncertain. Suzie walked to the door. "Hang tough," she repeated. "He can't make you go if you don't want to."

It sounded good.

The problem was, she had a feeling that somehow she would wind up going—and sticking out like a daisy at a rose convention.

Why wouldn't everyone just leave her alone?

"Ready?" Chris asked cheerfully, the moment she opened the door in response to his knock.

She all but glared at him, and snapped, "No!" in response.

His eyes skimmed over her. In his opinion, she looked ready. Gorgeous and ready. But he had sisters, so he knew all about not being ready despite appearances.

"Oh, okay." Walking in the door, Chris leaned casually against the wall. "I'll wait."

"In vain," she countered. She was aware that the words sounded combative.

Chris looked like the soul of innocence as he asked, "You're not really going to disappoint my uncle, are you?"

"No," she answered, and then, before he could misunderstand her meaning, she added, "because he won't even notice I'm not there. How could he?" she cried. "There'll be too many other people there. It's like saying he'd miss a grain of sand on the beach."

The look on O'Bannon's face told her he thought she was gravely oversimplifying the matter. "Oh,

Uncle Sean'll notice," he assured her with conviction. "You're underestimating his powers of observation."

She all but laughed in his face. "At last count, there were enough Cavanaughs and Cavanaughs-by-relation to fill a midsized football stadium. There's no way he'll notice that I'm not there—*if you don't bring it to his attention,*" she said, emphasizing each word.

Chris wasn't about to lie. He didn't believe in it. "Well, I'll have to if he asks."

She had the perfect solution to that. "Then stay out of his line of vision and he won't ask. There," she concluded. "Simple."

Chris laughed. He couldn't help it. She seemed adorably naive.

"Even if this 'plan' of yours works," he told her, "there's always Monday morning."

Suzie didn't understand. "Monday morning?"

"Yes. Monday morning. That's when he'll mention not having seen you. Probably first thing," Chris guessed. "What are you going to do then?"

Her exasperation had almost reached the breaking point. "Monday is two days away," she cried, throwing up her hands. "I'll come up with something by then."

"You know," O'Bannon told her after some deliberation, "you never struck me as being cowardly."

He was making her squirm inside. Any second she was going to be squirming on the outside, too.

"I'm not," she snapped.

"Good, my mistake," he said in a particularly chipper voice. "Then it's settled."

That was when he took her by the hand and began to draw her out the door. For a second, Suzie was stunned. He'd caught her off guard and had completely thrown her by taking her hand. It was the first real physical contact between them, and Suzie berated herself for the fact that she felt her pulse accelerating.

Annoyed with him and with herself, she yanked her hand away.

"I can walk," she informed him curtly.

"And I look forward to watching that," he told her, gesturing her in the general direction of his car. "By the way, you look nice."

"I look dressed," Suzie corrected tersely, since she felt that there was nothing particularly outstanding about what she had on.

"That's one way to describe it," he allowed, wanting to avoid getting into an argument with her if at all possible. "Now all you have to do is not look as if I'm leading you to your execution, and everything'll be just fine."

She made one last-ditch attempt. "I don't do well in crowds."

"Speaking on behalf of 'the crowd,' we don't want you to 'do' anything," he told Suzie. "We just want you to *be*."

"Be what?" she asked, when he didn't seem about to finish his sentence.

By now he'd gotten her all the way over to his car, which he'd left in the first spot in guest parking.

"Be," Chris repeated. "Just *be*, Suzie Q. As in *exist*. You know, I don't understand why you're so spooked about this," he told her quite honestly. "It's just a bunch of cops getting together. You're around cops every day," he pointed out.

"No," she contradicted stubbornly, "I'm in the lab every day. By myself. The cops come and go."

"The last couple of weeks have been different," he pointed out to her patiently. She knew that. She didn't need him to spell it out to her. "Honestly," he went on, "we don't bite. Not even my mother."

Suzie had gotten into his car, but froze as she was fastening her seat belt. "Your mother?"

He nodded, smoothly blending in with the rest of the traffic as he pulled out of the complex.

"As far as I know, she'll be there. She's one of those 'dreaded Cavanaughs.' By birth," Chris added cheerfully.

"Your mother," Suzie repeated, as if his words were barely sinking in.

"Yes. She'll be there. We've established that fact, Suzie Q. She's actually very nice," he told her. "I didn't think that for a few years back when I was in high school, but then my mother called those my 'wild years.'"

"And when will they be over, exactly?" Suzie asked sarcastically.

"Score one for the lab jockey," he said magnanimously. "Tell you what," he suggested as he drove the familiar route to the former chief of police's recently renovated and expanded house, "Give this get-together an hour. If you still feel like jumping ship, then we'll leave."

He was just saying that to get her to lower her guard.

"What if I can't find you in an hour?" Suzie challenged.

"You think I'm going to bail on you?" he asked, intrigued.

The man could make innocent look believable, she thought—except that she knew better. "Something like that."

"Not a chance, Suzie Q," he promised. "But if, for some reason, we *do* get separated—" he began.

"Ha!" Suzie declared, as if he'd just proved her point.

Chris never blinked. "I was going to say, send up a flare, I'll find you."

She sighed deeply. She could probably set her hair on fire and he'd pretend not to see her.

"This is a mistake."

"No," he retorted. "A mistake is not facing what you're afraid of—because if you don't face it, it'll haunt you forever."

"You sound like a fortune cookie," she said dismissively.

"That's too long to fit into a fortune cookie." Changing the subject as he turned into a residential development, he stated, "We're almost there."

Suzie blinked, surprised. She had no idea she lived so close to the former chief.

"This looks like a parking lot," she cried, when he drove onto the block where Andrew Cavanaugh lived. There were cars lining both sides of the street as far as she could see.

"Told you," Chris said, vindicated. "Carpooling is the only way to go."

"All these the people who drove these vehicles carpooled?" she asked incredulously. She'd lost count of the vehicles. "Just how many of you are there?"

"You can do an official head count when we get there if you want." He continued scanning the area, searching for an empty spot. "By the way, we're allowed to bring friends. Like you."

Suzie made no comment.

They found a space two blocks away—a block that had a large residential playground on it, which accounted for the free space. It meant they had a long walk to the house.

"I would have let you out by the front door," Chris told her as they exited the car, "but I was afraid you'd make a break for it."

"Is that what you actually thought?" she asked as they started toward their destination.

"Yes." He wondered if he'd just opened the door to another argument. Her response surprised him.

"You're smarter than you look," she was forced to admit.

Chris laughed and shook his head. "Looks like I'm not the only one who's going to have to brush up on their flattery skills," he observed, remembering what she'd said to him the other day.

"I know how to conduct myself around people." The look in his eyes was rather doubtful. She knew what he was thinking—which was a scary thought in itself. She chose not to dwell on it. "You're a different matter. You're not people."

He laughed as they reached the chief's block. "I'll take that as a compliment."

Suzie tossed her head, sending her hair swaying against her back like a sultry blond wave. "It wasn't meant to be."

"I know." His eyes glinted with humor. "But I'm taking it that way, anyway."

They had reached his uncle's front door, but rather than knock on it, Chris put his hand on the doorknob and began to turn it.

"Aren't you going to knock?" she asked, surprised that he was just going to walk in.

"Nobody'll probably hear," he told her. "They're a noisy bunch and they're too busy having fun." Gesturing for her to enter, he said with deliberate politeness, "After you."

"You're just afraid if you go first, I'll run off."

He merely smiled at her, still waiting for her to go first. "We do think alike," he agreed.

"Heaven forbid." With a sigh, she walked in.

Suzie became aware of the wall of noise, of blended voices the moment she walked into the house. She was also aware that more than a couple people glanced in their direction—and that they were all smiling as they nodded a greeting.

Most of all, she was aware of the warmth, both in temperature and in atmosphere. It was immediately evident that all these people got along and liked each other.

She could feel deep-seated apprehension rising to the surface.

How would they take her presence here? Yes, she was part of law enforcement, but she wasn't part of *them*. She was an interloper. People she'd known all her life, people who were more family to her than her own family, had turned their backs on her when it came to light that her father might have been the dreaded serial killer who had preyed on homeless women in and around their town. They didn't even wait until it was a proved fact, they just accepted it as gospel.

And then it had been hatred by association.

"You must be Chris's new partner." The deep rumbling voice and the older woman it belonged to ambushed her. She took Suzie's hands, her own soft and comforting, and giving Suzie an odd feeling of well-being when they made contact.

"I'm his long-suffering mother, Maeve," the woman introduced herself. "Maeve Cavanaugh O'Bannon."

Just slightly taller than Suzie, Maeve easily outweighed her by a good twenty, twenty-five pounds, all of which were evenly distributed to create the impression of a powerful woman who knew her own mind and who took no garbage from anyone, not her children and especially not her brothers.

"I'm not his partner," Suzie corrected politely. "We're just temporarily working together on a case."

Rather than looking annoyed at being corrected, Maeve took the words in stride. "Ah, my mistake. The way Chris talked, I thought you two were lifelong partners. How's the case coming along? Any closer to catching the bastard?" Maeve asked, sounding as if she was genuinely interested.

That was when Chris placed himself between them. "She didn't come here to talk shop, Ma. She came here to sample some of Uncle Andrew's famous cooking."

Maeve patted her arm, never missing a beat as she changed topics. "Prepare to have your taste buds think they've died and gone to heaven. If I'd grown up around this man, I'd be three times as large as I am now," she confided to Suzie with a broad wink.

And then she turned to her son. "Where are your manners, Christian? I didn't raise you in a closet. Take this girl and introduce her around to the others. Make her feel welcome, for heaven's sake." And then Maeve seemed to think better of her last instruction. "Never mind. That's our job," she decided.

He caught Suzie's urgent, if silent cry for help, and came to the rescue. "Give her some breathing space, Ma."

Although he loved his mother dearly, in his opinion she came on too strong.

"You want breathing space, take her outside,"

Maeve told him. "Your uncle's got the buffet table set up back there. You can get that precious breathing space and stuffed mushrooms at the same time," she told them. The next moment, Maeve O'Bannon had moved on.

"You okay?" Chris asked, leaning close to Suzie. When she nodded, he began to usher her out through the patio doors to the backyard. "Ma can be a little overwhelming at times," he confided. "But she means well."

Suzie was still trying to come to terms with something the older woman had said to her. "You told her about me?" she asked.

"I didn't go out of my way to say anything, but she likes being kept in the loop and calls me like once a week, same as she does the others," he said, referring to his siblings. Weekly calls even though they all lived close to one another was a given. It was how they stayed in touch. "You were part of the answer to 'How's your newest case going?'"

Suzie stared at him. "You talk to your mother once a week?" she asked incredulously.

"Sure. What's wrong with that?"

"Nothing, but I'd watch my back if I were you," she warned. "They might stick you in a museum."

"I take it you don't talk to your mother often."

She pressed her lips together, debating not saying anything at all. But he could find out if he wanted to. She had listed that in her background information. "Can't. She's been dead for three years."

Damn, he'd walked all over that, he thought, upbraiding himself.

"Oh, I'm sorry. I didn't mean to bring up old wounds. But that doesn't mean you can't talk to her," he told her. When Suzie looked at him as if he'd lost his mind, he was more than happy to set her straight. "I talk to my dad sometimes and he's been dead for a real long time."

She remembered him mentioning that a while ago. Suzie shook her head. "You are weird."

"So some people have said," he allowed with a laugh. "Let me lead you to the food and you'll forget all about how weird I am."

"That would take a *lot* of food," she cracked.

"Lucky for both of us, 'a lot' doesn't even begin to describe this spread."

Which was when she saw the buffet table—and discovered that the man beside her was actually given to understatement.

Chapter 16

True to his word, despite obviously having a good time with the members of his extended family, Chris resisted being drawn away by his cousins when they wanted to play a game of pool, or when Bryce wanted to take him for a ride to show him what his new sport car could do on the open road.

Instead, Chris O'Bannon never left Suzie's side. Not only that, but the man really did appear to be ready to leave the gathering whenever she indicated that she wanted to leave.

It wasn't anything that he said, but Suzie could feel it in the way he looked at her, the way he'd touch her shoulder as he ushered from one group to another when he wanted her to see something. And because Chris appeared to be so willing to take his cues from her, Suzie found herself progressively lowering her guard by small increments. Before long, she could feel herself relaxing and enjoying the company of these people, who all seemed to genuinely like one another and get along so well.

And just like that, before she realized it, she was having a really good time.

So much so that when it did come time to leave, she was amazed that so much time had gone by so quickly.

"Well, you survived the Cavanaugh clan en masse," Andrew Cavanaugh told her with a low, rumbling laugh as she and Chris were saying their goodbyes to him and his wife. A tall, imposing man, the former chief of police gave her a quick hug. "I think that speaks very well for your endurance ability."

"Don't listen to a word he says, dear," his wife, Rose, told her with a wink. "He thrives on this and goes out of his way to make sure that everyone has a good time. He wants to make sure you all keep coming back for more."

Andrew put on the same innocent face that Suzie had seen on Chris. "All I did was open my doors. Oh, and cooked," he added modestly, as if it was just an afterthought.

The chief wrapped his arm around his wife's shoulders. Even those who weren't aware of their back story—of what he had gone through to find Rose when a cruel act of fate had separated them, taking her away for years—could see that the man adored his wife, as she did him.

The unspoken affection between them seemed almost contagious, Suzie couldn't help thinking. She could have sworn it filled the very air.

"Everything was wonderful," she told the couple with enthusiasm. "Thank you for having me."

Andrew's eyes crinkled as pleasure etched his features. "Well, now that you know the way, don't be a stranger," he told her. Looking over her head, his eyes met Chris's. "See to it, Chris."

"I'll do my best, sir."

It was an automatic response. Chris knew damn well that he couldn't get the woman beside him to do anything she didn't want to. Today had been an unexpected triumph, one that he felt she really needed. But that had come about because of her promise to Sean. It didn't automatically mean Chris could get her to come back.

Escorting her out the door and down the residential blocks to where he had left his car, Chris seemed conspicuously quiet. Too quiet.

So much so that Suzie thought maybe she'd done something to annoy him at the gathering.

It wasn't like the talkative detective to keep to himself this way. It almost made her uneasy.

By the time they reached the car, she was about to demand to know what she'd done wrong to make him lapse into silence this way.

She never got the opportunity, because Chris

turned to her and asked, with amusement in his eyes, "So, did you have a good time?"

Denial wasn't even an option. Not that she wanted to, but then again, it was difficult to come right out and tell him that he'd been right in his prediction about today. Still, he deserved to know that she *did* have a good time. Besides, even if she didn't come right out and say it, her expression at the gathering must have been a dead giveaway.

"Yes."

He smiled, thoroughly enjoying his triumph. "I was right, wasn't I?"

"Yes," Suzie admitted, even though she *was* a tad reluctant to do so. "They're a really nice bunch of people."

"I think so," he told her.

Despite that brief conversation, the short ride home was spent in almost eerie silence. There wasn't even an exchange of small talk, because she had fallen silent, lost in another set of thoughts, descending into wishful thinking regarding something that she had absolutely no ability to change.

She knew why she was being quiet, but why was O'Bannon? she wondered as he pulled up into guest parking at her apartment complex.

Suzie slanted a glance in his direction when he pulled up the hand brake, but said nothing as they got out of his vehicle.

"I'll walk you home," he told her, when she looked at him quizzically.

This wasn't exactly a date, she argued to herself as

he began to walk beside her. It was more like just two coworkers attending a function together. He wasn't bound by any so-called dating etiquette.

"You don't have to," she told him.

"Sure I do," Chris quipped. "It's part of the package."

Reaching her door, Suzie couldn't remain silent any longer. She swung around to face him. "You know, don't you?"

"Know what?" he asked.

She blew out an exasperated breath. "Don't pretend to be dumb, O'Bannon. It doesn't suit you."

He smiled in response. "I think that's the nicest compliment you've ever given me."

"It's the only compliment I've ever given you," Suzie pointed out.

Chris inclined his head, giving her the point. "There's that, too."

She didn't understand. If he knew—and she was pretty sure he'd known ever since they questioned Eldridge—why had he kept it to himself? Why hadn't he confronted her with it?

"Why didn't you say anything?" she asked. Then before Chris could answer, because this wasn't the kind of conversation she wanted to have out in the open, even if it was after midnight and, from all appearances, all her neighbors were in for the night and most likely asleep, Suzie pushed open her door. "Would you like to come in for something to drink? I think I might have something vaguely alcoholic."

"Vaguely sounds good," he answered, following

her inside. He eased the door closed behind him, never taking his eyes off Suzie.

Meanwhile, she was taking inventory of her refrigerator and found an unopened bottle of red wine pushed all the way to the back. She held it up for his benefit. "I have this, orange juice and diet soda," she told him.

He made his selection. "Wine—as long as you have some with me."

"Fair enough."

Bottle in hand, she went in search of a corkscrew. She found it in the top drawer of the kitchen cabinet, after rummaging through an assortment of things she'd meant to throw out. Turning around, she held the corkscrew and bottle out to him. She wasn't all that good at removing corks.

"Want to do the honors?" she asked.

Taking them, Chris quickly separated the cork from the bottle, then passed both back to her. "You don't strike me as a wine drinker," he mused.

Taking out two fluted glasses—the only two she had—Suzie poured a little wine into each. "I'm not."

Chris accepted the glass she handed him. "Then why have some in the house?"

Suzie shrugged as they went to sit on her sofa. After kicking off her heels, she tucked her feet beneath her.

"In case my brother ever decided to hop a plane and pay a visit. He likes wine," she confided. They were back to the subject that had caused her to invite him into her apartment to begin with. Suzie repeated her question. "Why didn't you say anything?"

"Well, it wasn't exactly the easiest topic to just start talking about out of the blue," he stated.

She thought of the people in her town, the individuals she'd viewed, up to that point, as friends. "Other people would." There was bitterness in her voice.

And then her mind went to Warren Eldridge. Had she not cut him dead the way she had when he'd called her a different name than the one she gave him, it was apparent the billionaire would have asked her all sorts of probing questions.

"That's for you to talk about—or not talk about," Chris told her. He never took his eyes off her as he sipped his wine.

Suzie stared into her glass, but didn't raise it to her lips. All sorts of emotions were churning within her. "You are an unusual man, Christian O'Bannon."

He laughed as he set down his wineglass. "I've been trying to tell you that."

"You were right," she told him. "I did have a good time. And I did need that—to attend a party and be around a normal family." She looked at him. "But I think you knew that, too."

He shrugged, making no comment on her observation. "Well, I think that might be stretching the meaning of the word *normal*."

"Not really," Suzie replied. "You've got good people in your family. And there's no danger of finding out that one of them is actually a serial killer," she added, her voice quavering. Struggling to regain control, she closed her eyes.

"You don't have to talk about this if you don't want to, Suzie Q," Chris told her softly. He felt for her, he really did. He couldn't begin to imagine what that must have been like, to discover that the man she'd loved and called "Dad" all her life was a monster she couldn't begin to recognize.

She opened her eyes and looked at him. "You know, that's the first time you've said my name where I haven't wanted to punch you."

He smiled at her. "I guess that means we're making progress."

Suzie sighed, remembering. Both hating and, yes, loving the man she was talking about. "He really acted like such a nice man, you know. My father," she added, in case O'Bannon thought she was referring to someone in his family.

"I know," he told her, his tone quietly encouraging her to continue—but only if she wanted to.

She started to talk, to unload. "My father was a textbook model dad. He never raised his voice, never missed church. He coached my brother's Little League team, was a Scout leader. The neighborhood kids adored him. He took us on camping trips. Eric Quinlan was the perfect husband, the perfect father, the perfect everything. Until he wasn't."

Tears of anger and hurt began to fill her eyes. "We never saw it coming. None of us. It was right there in front of us and none of us ever had a clue what he was doing. What kind of a monster he was."

Chris put his hand over hers. He doubted that she was even aware of him doing so, but he wanted to comfort her somehow. "No one else did, either."

"But they weren't his family," she insisted, looking up at him. "That was what everyone in town said when the case broke and the bodies just kept on turning up and up." She pressed her hand to her stomach. "For a while, it didn't look as if it was ever going to stop. And everyone, just *everyone,* kept asking, 'How could you not have known what he was doing?'" She pressed her lips together, keeping a sob back. "That's what I keep asking myself. How could I not have seen it? How could I not have known what he was doing all those years?"

"We see what we think we see," Chris told her, "Don't beat yourself up about it, Suzie. Your father was an expert at deception, at living two lives. If he hadn't been, his other life would have been exposed a long time ago."

She was crying openly now. She hadn't actually cried since the news about her father's serial killings had broken. She'd kept a steel-like hold on her emotions all through the trial, her mother's suicide, everything. Suzie was terrified that if she loosened her grip just a little, she would fall completely apart.

The way she was doing right now.

When Chris took her into his arms, she immediately resisted. She tried hard to push him away, to somehow regain her self-control and keep everything at bay, the way she had these last three years.

But he persevered, holding her until she stopped

fighting and slumped again him, letting the tears come. She didn't know how long she cried like that, and how long he just held her without a word. But eventually, her tears subsided.

Moving her head back just enough to look up at him, she murmured, "I'm sorry."

"For what?" he asked. "For being human? Don't be. I'll let you in on a little secret. The rest of us are human, too."

"Why are you being so nice to me?" she cried. After all, she'd been nasty to him on so many occasions, given him a hard time over and over again. This would be a perfect time for him to exact revenge if he wanted to.

"Have to," Chris told her. "I left my whip in the trunk of my car."

It was a perfectly ridiculous statement. She had no idea why it struck her as being so funny.

Or why, once she began to laugh, she just continued to, unable to stop. But she did. She laughed so hard that there were tears in her eyes, tears of laughter to mingle with her tears of anguish and pain.

Then finally, she began to get some control over herself. Suzie let out a shaky breath.

"You must think I'm crazy," she told him.

Chris shook his head. "Nope, don't think that, either."

She took a deep breath, trying to steady herself. She still felt as if she was coming undone, and dragged a hand through her hair. "I must look like a mess."

"Not possible," he told her, reaching into his back pocket and taking out his handkerchief. "Just a little wet, but I can fix that," he added with a smile.

Very carefully, his eyes on hers, he began to wipe away the tears from her cheeks. "See," he murmured, still wiping, "better already."

The last word faded on his tongue as he drew closer to her, being pulled by the look in her eyes, by the very real desire that had suddenly risen out of nowhere and seized him.

Before he knew exactly how it happened, Chris found himself lowering his mouth to hers and kissing her. Kissing away her pain.

Cupping her face between his hands, still sitting beside Suzie on the sofa, he deepened the kiss. The next thing he knew, he had pulled her closer to him, taking her into his arms as if he had been waiting his entire life to do just this very thing: to bind his soul to hers.

She was vulnerable. Anyone looking at her could see that in an instant. What kind of a man would he be to take advantage of that?

With what felt like the last ounce of his strength, Chris put his hands on her shoulders and held her away from him.

"Suzie," he cautioned. "You don't want to do this."

She felt bewildered and not a little dizzy and stunned. "I don't?"

He tried again. "I mean, you don't want to do something you're going to regret."

"Then don't make me regret it," she whispered,

taking hold of the front of his shirt and pulling him back to her.

The next moment, her mouth was sealed to his. The time for discussion was over.

Chapter 17

Chris had never been one to be ruled by his emotions. He responded to them when it suited him, but he never allowed himself to be ruled by them. He'd always made it a point to be in charge of his own actions and ultimately, his own feelings. Thus he'd never had that feeling that he was being taken for a ride.

Until this time.

This time it was different.

This time, Chris could have sworn that he had caught a huge tidal wave and that he'd gotten swept up in its crest.

Just inhaling the fragrance that he detected in her hair and along her skin made his blood rush so quickly that he felt dizzy.

Chris responded to her without any clear thought accompanying his actions.

As he pulled Suzie even closer than he already had, his lips left hers. Moving aside the tiny gold cross she always wore, he began to kiss the slope of her neck and then to imprint a network of kisses along the swell of her breasts.

Desire continued to build within him rather than being satiated. The more he lost himself in her, the more he wanted to be lost. The sound of her heavy breathing stoked the fire in his veins, making him want to possess her the way he'd never really wanted to possess another woman. Utterly and completely.

It wasn't enough for him just to make love with her. Chris wanted to make her want him, to make her feel these pounding needs that were assaulting his own body, and reciprocate in kind.

What began almost politely escalated at the rate of a raging forest fire that had gone completely out of control.

Everywhere he touched her just seemed to heighten his desire tenfold. He'd fallen down an abyss and there was no bottom, no end in sight.

He didn't care. As long as they were here together, nothing else mattered.

Suzie's head began to spin the first moment his breath touched her skin, even before Chris kissed her. And once he had, there was no turning back for her, even though a part of her watched, stunned and awed at what was transpiring right before her.

Right *within* her.

She'd never reacted to a man this way before, never gotten to this stage with one. She'd never *felt* like this about a man, never experienced the need or desire to have this happen. Love, romance, lovemaking—they were things that happened to other people, not her. And because there had been no intense feelings present, there had never been any reason or need for things to go this far.

Before the scandal revolving around her father had hit, when her life was simpler, she'd never found anyone who made her heart skip a beat, much less beat faster. It wasn't that she wasn't interested in finding love, just that no one had attracted her enough to make love a reality.

After the scandal, she'd been so caught up in guarding her feelings, in keeping the world and all its hurtful words at arm's length, Suzie had refused to entertain the very idea of having love in her life.

But right from the start, there had been something about this man, who was cocky and sweet at the same time, who butted heads with her and then put his arm around her. Something about Chris O'Bannon broke through every single protective defense mechanism she had put in place to shield her from the pain she was certain was waiting for her.

That he had gone to the trouble of unearthing her secret and yet hadn't confronted her with it had been the last straw—and the winning coup. He'd quite simply won her heart—or whatever she had left that still passed for a heart—with that one single action. That one act of kindness.

All along, she had been fighting what she both felt and knew was inevitable: her attraction to him. And tonight, when he'd brought her home, it had overpowered her and she had just allowed that feeling to take over.

She had surrendered.

Succumbing to those feelings, Suzie began to tug at his clothing even before he began to unzip her sundress.

While she worked away at the uncooperative buttons on Chris's shirt, struggling to get them through the holes, she shivered as she suddenly felt the zipper slowly being coaxed down her spine. It kept sliding lower until her sundress slipped off her shoulders and then down her body, descending to the floor like a sigh.

Having finally gotten Chris's shirt off, she pressed her body against his. She didn't remember how or when she'd managed to get his pants off, but she was acutely aware of the clasp on her bra being deftly undone and the wispy garment joining her dress on the floor.

Other underwear quickly melded with the scattered clothing. Body parts slid against one another as kiss after hungry kiss caused her desire to accelerate, echoing the wild pounding of her heart.

So this is what it's all about, Suzie thought in awe. *The noise, the songs, the endless quest that others undertake for the sake of this fantastic feeling build-*

ing in my veins. Words didn't begin to do it justice, she realized, trying to capture, to savor as much as she could from the experience, from the moment.

From the man.

She was on fire, Chris thought, and so was he.

Like the very air, Suzie seemed to be everywhere, kissing him, touching him, sliding her body along his and creating nothing short of a burning, all-consuming need for that final moment, that heady, overwhelming rush when the surge erupted.

She was incredible.

He could honestly say he'd never been with anyone like Suzie before. Supple, eager, breathtakingly limber, she was very nearly wiping him out.

But if that was the case, he really couldn't think of a better way to go.

Their bodies were entangled on her oversize sofa, and Chris grasped her hands in one of his as he laced one last trail of kisses along her body, this time going down even farther than he had initially. So far that he heard her cry out in wonder as well as intense pleasure.

When he lifted his head, he saw that she appeared close to ecstasy. That was when he raised himself up, sliding along her damp body until his eyes were level with hers. Capturing her hands again, this time one in each of his, he moved his knee until she parted her legs for him.

Then, still intently watching her, his own heart hammering, he began to slip into her.

And then abruptly stopped.

She saw the puzzled look, the unspoken question, and knew if she didn't do something quickly, he was going to back away from her.

From this.

She couldn't bear that, couldn't bear being abandoned.

So she raised her hips urgently, pushing against him until Chris had no will left, no recourse but to continue what he had started: the dance of the ages that for tonight was theirs alone.

She bit back the cry of pain that rose in her throat, swallowing it as she continued to move with him, increasing the urgent tempo with each moment that passed until they were both frantically rushing to journey's end, each holding fast to the other so that they would reach it together.

She shivered as she felt it, felt the implosion that shook her to her very core as supreme pleasure cascaded through her, bringing with it peace and a sense of satisfaction she had never known before.

Suzie collapsed beneath him, breathing hard.

Incredibly content.

Spent, Chris rolled off her.

So many emotions were storm-trooping through him, he couldn't begin to catalog them. But foremost, he was angry, and felt like getting up and putting distance between them until he could get control over this fury throbbing within him.

But another part of him reminded Chris that this woman had been abandoned enough and he couldn't allow himself to hurt her. Because that first reaction was temporary, fleeting. Something else, something beneath it, was far, far stronger.

So instead, Chris remained where he was, and because being cold and withdrawn was not something he did well, after a moment's hesitation, he drew her to him and held her.

"Something else you didn't tell me," he said. It wasn't a question, but more of a wearily stated accusation.

She'd seen the surprise in his eyes a moment before she'd physically forced him to continue. There was no point in pretending that she didn't know what he was talking about.

She did.

So she searched for something to say, but absolutely nothing was coming to mind. How did one respond to something liked that?

"Why didn't you tell me?" Chris asked.

"I was thinking of having cards printed up so I could pass them out, but I just couldn't make up my mind about the font," she told him, her face completely unreadable. And then her voice grew very, very serious as she asked, "Just how was I supposed to work that into the conversation? And when? While we were talking to your uncle? Or maybe when you introduced me to your mother? 'Hi, I'm Susannah Quinn, I work for your brother in the CSI lab and, oh, yes, by the way, I'm a virgin. When I'm not at the lab, I have a little cubicle at the Museum of Natural History. Mine is right next to the one where they keep the unicorn, another mythical creature.'"

Suzie shook her head as she got up off the couch. "Sorry, I just couldn't find the proper place to drop that little ticking bomb. I'm sorry if you're disappointed," she told him, snatching up her clothes and holding them against her. She wanted to make her getaway, to slip into the bathroom and stay there until he left.

But Chris grabbed her wrist, holding her in place. "Who said anything about being disappointed?" he asked.

"Well, isn't that why you're so angry with me?" she demanded.

It was hard for him to put his feelings about this into words. He'd never been in this kind of a situation before, never been anyone's "first." He'd just taken it for granted that someone Suzie's age, that someone who *looked* like Suzie, would have had her share of lovers.

"I look so angry," he explained, "because it would have been nice to have had a little prior warning before I found myself 'barging in' like some kind of Neanderthal."

She raised her chin defensively, determined not to cry. "Why? So you could walk out?"

"No, you idiot," he snapped. Didn't she understand what kind of position she'd put him in? How bad he felt about this? "So I could go a little slower. Your first time shouldn't feel like it was some kind of race to the finish line. It should be something that happened in stages, slowly, to get your body ready for what was happening."

She was doing her best to understand. What she *did* understand was that he didn't regret what happened because she was inexperienced. He regretted it because had he known, he would have wanted to make the experience better for her.

"I don't think it would have been humanly possible for my body to be any more ready," she told him. "And if you feel that bad about it, well," she told him, a whimsical smile playing on her lips, "I wouldn't really mind a do-over."

He laughed and pulled her into his arms. "You can't 'do over' a first time, Suzie Q."

"No," she agreed. "But there's no reason why there shouldn't be a second attempt. To get it right, you understand," she added, her eyes shimmering with humor.

He shifted in one smooth motion, so that Suzie was beneath him on the sofa. The fact that she had, until a few minutes ago, been a virgin was still gnawing at him. It didn't make any sense.

"How is it that no one ever made love to you before, Suzie Q?"

She smiled up into his eyes. "No one was ever fast enough to catch me before."

"And I was?" he questioned, amused by her explanation.

She seemed to consider her answer. "Or maybe you just got lucky because I got tired of running."

"You got that right," he told her. He saw her eyebrow arch, as if she wasn't following him. "I got lucky." With that, he lowered his mouth to hers. "We'll go slower this time," he promised as he started to kiss her again.

Chris heard her laugh, *tasted* her laugh as it rumbled against his lips.

"Good luck with that," she told him.

And within a moment, he saw what she meant.

She set the pace and it was even more frantic than it had been the first time.

Keeping up with her was not easy, but he found that it was probably the most delightful exercise in near futility he'd ever endured.

It didn't keep him from trying.

And when it was over and they lay beside one another with only the sound of their heavy breathing cutting through the silence in the room, Chris discovered that he had to struggle to get his pulse back under control.

Another first, he couldn't help thinking.

"Thirty-eight seventy-seven Alexander Street," he managed to gasp when he could finally find enough breath to form words.

She turned her head to face him, completely lost. "What's...that?"

"The address...to...my mother's house. It's... where I want you...to send my remains. She'll want to give me...a proper burial."

Mystified, Suzie propped herself up on her elbow, although it wasn't easy. "*What* are you talking about?" she asked.

"You wore me out, Suzie Q," he told her, then took another deep breath before he added, "One more time and I'm done for."

"Is that a dare?" she asked, a smile playing on her lips.

"Just a statement." Chris turned his body toward hers. "Make of it what you will."

"What I make of it," she told him, doing her best to gather herself together, "is that it's a dare, and I never walk away from a dare."

"You have a lot in common with my sister Shayla," he said.

Suzie moved so that she was right over him. "I'm not your sister."

"Thank heaven for small favors," he murmured, just as her lips were about to cover his.

And then his cell phone rang.

For a moment, they both tried to ignore it. But law enforcement was too ingrained in both of them. When it rang again, Chris sighed, sat up and reached for the device, which was on the floor next to the sofa.

"Maybe it's a wrong number," he said to Suzie, just before he swiped open his phone and said, "O'Bannon."

"We've got another body."

Chapter 18

"Technically, you know," Chris said to her, "this isn't our body."

"That sounds like the beginning of a territorial battle between two zombies," Suzie said with a laugh. "Not exactly the kind of pillow talk I expected after my first time."

After the call came in and Chris had gotten the particulars, they had hurriedly dressed and hit the road. They were now heading for the destination the detective who'd phoned had specified.

"That's what you get for taking up with a homicide detective. And by the way, somebody is watching way too much cable," Chris commented. "Zombies? Really?"

"I've just seen the commercials. I don't watch the

shows," she told him. "Way too creepy for my tastes." Suzie redirected the conversation to the reason they weren't still in her apartment, working up energy for another go-round. "Exactly where is this body located?"

He told her what his friend had told him. "In a deserted building in Quail Hill."

Suzie expressed minor surprise. "I wasn't aware that they *had* any deserted buildings in Quail Hill. It's so upscale." Just a hint of a smile curved her lips. "I thought it wasn't allowed."

Chris took the freeway. It was quicker at this hour of the early morning. "Apparently someone neglected to read the bylaws," he quipped.

She had another question for him. "So why are we going there if the murder happened out of our jurisdiction?"

"Because I knew you'd want to see the scene," he told her honestly. While he wouldn't call her obsessed, he knew that she was determined to catch the killer, and everybody they studied brought them that much closer to their man. "I put the word out to some of my connections in a few neighboring cites, asking to be notified if they get any victims where the perp used the same MO as our serial killer did."

"O'Bannon, I think you just won my heart," she told him.

"That was my intent." She looked at him, trying to decide if he was just being funny, or if there was some germ of truth to his comment. "That and catching the SOB," he concluded, as he weaved to the far right lane just before exiting the freeway.

"Looks like it's the same guy," she agreed, when Paul Langford, the detective who had called Chris, pulled back the sheet from the woman who had just been discovered. Squatting beside the body, Suzie focused on the bruising along the dead woman's neck. "The victim's in her twenties, blonde, slender and exceptionally pretty."

"And ripe," Chris added, putting his hand in front of his nose. The stench was difficult to take. "How long has she been here?"

Suzie knew he wasn't asking her to guess. He was relying on her professional expertise.

"I'd say probably three, four days," she told him, standing up.

She looked around. The entire area was filled with freshly cut lumber and all the building materials that were necessary to transform what had once been a high-end supermarket into something far more upscale. From the looks of it, the girl's body had been hidden beneath the lumber.

Suzie shook her head. "Well, this definitely doesn't appear like anyone threw a party here recently." She turned toward Langford. "Who found her?" she asked the older detective.

"One of the construction crew came in early this morning to make sure everything was here so they could start work first thing tomorrow. The second he saw her, he called 911." There were several uniformed police on the grounds and one civilian. Langford pointed in the construction worker's general direction. "He's the really pale guy over there. Careful. You ask him too many questions and he's liable to start retching again. Missed my shoes by an inch," he added, indicating his footwear. "He didn't really have all that much to say when he wasn't retching."

"Do you have an ID on her yet?" Chris asked. From what he could see, there was no sign of a struggle, so this latest victim, like the others, must have been killed somewhere else.

"No place to put a wallet. She's naked," Langford pointed out. The detective appeared to be dead serious despite the ludicrousness of his comment. "That's what made me think she might have met up with your killer. He pretty much strips them down, right?"

Suzie took another, closer look at the victim's neck, doing her best not to breathe. The young woman had definitely been strangled. And just like with the other victims, the killer had used his hands.

Suzie knew this wasn't personal, but she couldn't help thinking that the killer was thumbing his nose at them. Taunting them, as if he felt certain he could keep getting away with it.

Her own father had probably felt the same way. Until he had apparently gotten overconfident and made one stupid mistake.

"It certainly looks like the work of the same man," she commented.

Langford regarded the dead woman thoughtfully.

"I can't release the body to you," he told them. "But what I can do is have our ME send you the autopsy report once it's done. You have any suspects yet?" he asked hopefully.

Chris was quick to answer before Suzie could say anything. "We're looking at a couple of people," he stated. "We'll let you know how it goes."

"You do that." Langford shook his head as he covered the young woman's face again. "A real waste," he murmured under his breath, then looked up at the two of them. "I don't mind telling you that I could use all the help I can get. This is all kind of new to me," he admitted freely. "She's our first murder in Quail Hill in more than seven years and I'd like to clean this up as soon as possible."

"Like I said, as soon as we know, you'll know," Chris promised. Taking Suzie's arm, he ushered her toward the exit. "Thanks again for giving us a heads-up," he called over his shoulder.

Suzie said nothing as they left the building. But once they were outside, walking back to Chris's vehicle, she couldn't keep quiet any longer. "Why didn't you tell him?"

"What?" he asked, hitting the remote device to unlock the doors. "That we might have a suspect?"

"That it's Eldridge," she stressed.

He got into the car. Suzie was already yanking on her seat belt. "Because we don't know," Chris pointed out patiently. "Because if we said we're considering the possibility that the serial killer might be Warren Eldridge—"

"Not 'might be,' it *is*," Suzie insisted adamantly.

He knew she believed what she was saying, and maybe she was starting to convince him, but they were a long way from being able to actually prove what her "gut" was telling her.

"Most people tend to give nationally renowned philanthropists a pass when it comes to accusing them of being serial killers."

As far as she was concerned, the philanthropist thing was an act, a cover that allowed Eldridge to do what he wanted to do—attract willing women who fit a certain description.

"Are you giving him a pass?" she questioned.

"I'm a big fan of evidence, Suzie Q, which is something we still need to get," Chris reminded her. He could literally feel her scowling. "I'm willing to question the man again, but remember, we can't just accuse him without proof."

She knew that. But it didn't negate the way she felt. "I *know* it's him. In my gut, I know it's him."

"As adorable as I think your gut is," Chris told her, "I'm afraid that it's just not enough proof to present in front of a jury."

Suzie felt so frustrated. It was like looking at journey's end with a huge chasm in the way. "We know that girl back there was his type."

"Correction," Chris pointed out, "she was the *serial killer's* type."

"I pulled up every single photo taken of that man at those fund-raisers he's always throwing. There's a tall, twentysomething, rail-thin blonde hanging off his arm in more than half of them."

Chris turned off his headlights. Daylight had become part of the landscape. "Still doesn't mean he's our killer."

"He is," Suzie insisted. "I know he is."

After taking a sharp right, Chris drove along the main thoroughfare that would bring them to the precinct. "Then we need to get the evidence to prove it," he told her calmly. "We need to build a case."

She clenched her hands in her lap. "Meanwhile, that grinning, worthless piece of garbage goes on killing."

Chris put his hand on top of hers for a moment, giving them a squeeze. "We'll build fast," he said. "C'mon, I'll buy you breakfast and then we'll start building. Deal?"

"Deal," she agreed grudgingly. "But make the breakfast to go."

He laughed. "You always have to have the final word, don't you?"

A glimmer of a smile slipped over her lips. "Is there any other kind?"

He laughed again. "Not when it comes to you."

Suzie ate at her desk, absently taking a bite every now and then, completely focused on going through the list of dead women they had previously put together. She was searching for connections beyond the obvious: that the victims all resembled one another enough to have been sisters.

Right now she was looking for one thing in particular—Warren Eldridge's whereabouts during the time of each murder.

"Take a break, Suzie Q," Chris finally said several hours later. Her French toast—there was more than half left—had gone soggy. He cleared it away and saw that she didn't even notice. "You've been at this for hours now. Any longer and I'm worried that you might forget how to walk."

"I think I've got something," Suzie announced suddenly, looking up.

Chris thought better of the snappy wisecrack that rose to his lips, and merely said, "Go ahead."

"I plotted a chart for each one of these murder victims, listing their approximate time of death," she began.

He heard the excitement in her voice. She was building up to something. He really hoped that it could stand up in court.

"And?"

The look of triumph on her face was impossible to miss. "And guess who was in town each and every time one of these women was murdered?"

"Offhand, I'd say probably several hundred people," Chris answered.

"Did I mention *every one* of the murders?" Suzie asked.

She wasn't going to let go of this, was she? Chris had to admit that he was growing somewhat concerned. "Okay," he amended, "a handful."

She wished he was more supportive. Still, she supposed she could see his side of it. His family made up the skeletal structure of the police department and one misstep could be blown completely out of proportion, causing a lot of them a great deal of trouble.

But then again, this wasn't a misstep, she silently insisted.

She laid it out for him. "Each and every time one of these bodies was found, Warren Eldridge was in the same city, either attending a fund-raiser or dedicating a scholarship to a local university, or at some award ceremony given in his honor."

"Makes it hard to sneak out," Chris said.

"With enough people milling around one of these places, he could easily slip out," Suzie contradicted. "And then slip back in. Who would really notice?"

Chris shook his head. "Still a coincidence."

"Oh, come on," Suzie cried. "Twice is a coincidence. Eleven times is definitely something else."

He'd hoped that they would find something definitely incriminating. "All right, if it makes you feel better, we'll go talk to him again now."

She shut off her computer and pushed her chair away from the desk. "What would make me feel better is nailing his butt to the wall."

Chris was already on his feet. "I don't think they make a tool for that."

"I'll improvise," she told him fiercely as they walked out of the office.

Warren Eldridge's assistant led them to the CEO's office, all the while telling them that they were going to have to state their business quickly.

"His flight is due out," the assistant informed them coldly just before he exited.

The first thing they saw were two suitcases, flanking what appeared to be an old-fashioned steamer trunk whimsically covered with aged, yellowed travel stickers. It seemed completely out of keeping with the image the man usually conveyed.

Eldridge was clearly a man in a hurry. But that didn't keep him from giving them a little time.

"Ah, Detectives. Have you come to tell me that you've caught that awful person who killed that poor, unfortunate girl?" he asked. "The one you found in the wake of the bash I attended?" he added, when neither answered his question.

Chris put his hand on Suzie's wrist, indicating that he was fielding the questions. He didn't want her saying anything for the time being.

"Not yet," he said. He waved a hand at the luggage. "Are you going somewhere?"

"I'm always going somewhere," Eldridge informed him with an easy laugh. "But specifically, I'm about to fly to New York. Ribbon-cutting ceremony," he explained. "They're opening a new cancer wing at Manhattan Hospital. Since I underwrote most of it, they insisted on dedicating it to the memory of my mother, Jacquelyn Eldridge. They've asked me to attend. So naturally, I said yes, but I have to leave within the half hour. Perforce, I'm afraid our visit is going to have to be short," he informed them. "So, did you catch him?"

"No, but there's been another murder," Chris told the man.

Eldridge looked properly appalled. "Really, Detectives, you have got to catch this heinous person," he exclaimed.

The man really irritated the hell out of her. Every word out of his mouth was like fingernails going down a chalkboard.

"You need to get your designations straight, Mr. Eldridge," Suzie informed him. "Detective O'Bannon is a detective. I, on the other hand, am a crime scene investigator."

Eldridge looked at her innocently. "Well, isn't investigating a crime scene, by definition, acting like a detective?" he asked.

"To get to the point," Chris said, cutting in before Suzie started hurling accusations at the man, "were you in Quail Hill recently?"

Eldridge didn't even pause to think. "You know I was, *Detective*," he replied, with deliberate emphasis, "or you wouldn't be here with your crime scene investigator."

"Do you have someone who could account for your whereabouts on—"

Eldridge cut him short. "I have any of a number of administrative assistants trailing after me at all hours, so I dare say that I could—" A ring tone coming from Chris's phone interrupted what the billionaire was about to say next. He waved a hand. "I'll wait if you want to get that."

Chris frowned as he pulled out his phone. Ordinarily, he'd ignore the ring tone. It was the one that alerted him a text was coming in. But since it might be something about the current case, he paused to look at the screen.

He read the words that had just appeared along the top, and everything around him seemed to freeze. Chris swiped his thumb along the lower edge of his phone, opening it. He read the rest of the text.

Suzie saw the look on his face and knew something was horribly wrong. "What is it?"

Numb, he raised his eyes to hers. "It's from Shayla," he said, referring to one of his sisters. "My mother's been in an accident."

Suzie's mouth dropped open. "You need to go," she told him. She saw Chris look at the man they were questioning, and knew what he was thinking. "Don't worry, I'll take it from here," she said. "You just go to your mother, make sure she's all right. Take the car," she added. She could see he was about to protest. "I'll get a ride when I finish with Mr. Eldridge here."

"She's right, Detective. You need to go see about your mother," Eldridge urged kindly.

Suzie saw the man glance at a wall where photographs of an incredibly beautiful woman were hung. For the first time, Suzie noticed that there was a small boy standing in the background in all of them.

"We only get one mom. I can drop your partner off at the precinct. It's on my way to my private airport," the man offered.

Chris clearly appeared torn. Taking his arm, Suzie

ushered him to one side, out of Eldridge's earshot. "He's leaving town. This might be the only chance we'll get to question him, otherwise I'd go with you. Don't worry about me, I'll catch up when I can—and I promise I won't slug him," she added, in case that was Chris's concern. "But right now, he still has questions to answer. Go. Go," she urged, all but pushing Chris out the door. "You're not going to do either one of us any good here. Your mind's not going to be on this, anyway."

Chris hesitated for a moment longer, but his concern got the better of him. "Call me the second you've finished questioning him," he told her.

"And you call me as soon as you see your mother. I know she's fine," Suzie added, knowing it was what he needed to hear.

Chris was gone in an instant.

Turning back to face Eldridge, she saw an odd expression on the man's face. For the life of her, she couldn't quite read it.

"It's touching to see such family devotion in this day and age. You don't often see it anymore," he told her.

The man made her blood run cold. She didn't care what Chris said about evidence; she knew she was right. She just had to prove it.

"They're an unusual family," she replied, never taking her eyes off Eldridge. Despite all the accolades she'd read about him, he still made her think of a reptile.

"That they are," he agreed, moving closer to her.

"All such dedicated public servants, as well. Maybe a little too dedicated, perhaps," he suggested. "I would think that Detective O'Bannon would have gotten his mother to retire by now instead of still driving that ambulance around."

Suzie remembered Chris correcting her when she'd said that. "His mother doesn't drive an ambulance, she oversees—" Suzie stopped abruptly. Something was off. "How do you know what she does?"

"I always do my homework when it comes to the people I interact with." His eyes pinned hers. She had the distinct impression that she was looking into the gaze of a cobra. "Just like I knew about what your father did. And how your mother thought that the only way to get away from that shame was to commit suicide. I like finding out people's secrets. Everyone has secrets, Susannah." He kept advancing. "For instance, my mother's secret was that she pretended she was a religious, devoted mother, when nothing could have been further from the truth."

For every step he took toward her, Suzie took one step back, all the while making sure she was moving toward the door.

"And what's your secret, Mr. Eldridge?" she challenged.

The smile on his lips almost made her heart stop. And all the while he kept coming closer. "Oh, I think you already know."

Pivoting on her heel, Suzie turned to run. She nearly made it to the door.

Her hand was on the doorknob when she felt it. Felt this strange pricking sensation at the side of her neck.

Her legs suddenly turned to lead.

And just before she fell to the floor, everything turned pitch-black.

Chapter 19

His mother had never had an accident, not so much as a fender bender or even a dent, in all the years she'd been driving, and that included when she drove an ambulance full-time for a living.

As far as he knew, she hadn't even had an accident when she was a teenager. If she had, his uncles would have been more than happy to rag on her and tell him.

It didn't make any sense.

Neither did the fact that she had been driving an ambulance at all. What kind of circumstances had to have transpired to get his mother behind the wheel of an ambulance again?

Maeve O'Bannon didn't drive ambulances anymore; she hadn't for years now. She was in charge of a fleet of four ambulances that were contracted to the city's fire department. She liked being a manager, liked it far better than jockeying through local traffic, half the time racing against the clock to get an injured person to the ER.

Now she *was* the injured person.

Maybe something had happened and his mother had wound up being a driver short. He knew his mom. If enough calls came in, she wouldn't reroute the call. She'd step up and drive the rig herself.

He couldn't allow his imagination to get carried away. He wasn't going to overthink this. His mother was fine, just fine. She was pretty damn close to invincible. Had been for as far back as he could remember.

Chris clutched the steering wheel, his knuckles white.

Damn it, how had this happened?

"And where the hell are you driving?" he asked himself out loud. Shayla's text hadn't told him which hospital his mother had been taken to.

Fumbling, Chris hit one of the top numbers that was programmed into his cell, then put his phone on speaker so he wouldn't have to strain to hear once the call was picked up.

The sound of ringing began to irritate him.

He counted off the number of rings. *One, two, three, four—*

Damn it, where was she? Why wasn't his sister answering? Shayla had just texted him less than five minutes ago. So why wasn't she picking up her phone?

Did that mean that—?

Hearing a noise over the line, Chris instantly became alert.

"This is Shay and you guessed it, I'm away, so leave your name and number and if you're lucky, I'll give you a call back."

Damn, he hated answering machines, he thought angrily. "Pick up, Shay! This is no time to play games. Pick up or so help me—"

This time, he heard an actual person picking up.

"Wow, wake up on the wrong side of the cave this morning, big brother?" his sister asked. His anger was all but vibrating through the cell.

Chris didn't waste any time telling her that he thought she was being callously flippant. He was afraid that every second counted. "Where is she?"

There was silence on the other end before Shayla finally asked, "Where's who?"

He blew out an angry breath. Was she being deliberately obtuse?

"The hospital—give me the name of the hospital." He swerved at the last moment, nearly hitting a minivan that was going way too slowly. "I'm en route and I need the name of the hospital she's in."

"What are you talking about?" Shayla cried. "What hospital?"

He was beginning to think his sister was in shock—either that, or in denial. Chris ground out each word. "The one they took Ma to."

"They took Mom to the hospital?" she asked in surprise. "When? Who?" She shot the questions out like gunfire, instantly concerned.

What was wrong with her? His sister was acting as if she didn't know anything about it. "You're the one who texted me about the accident," he cried.

"No, I didn't. I didn't even know she was in an accident." And then suddenly, some of the fear left her voice, to be replaced by genuine anger. "Chris, I swear, if this is some kind of an idiotic prank you're playing, it's not funny—"

"You didn't text me?" he demanded. He could feel his stomach seizing up as his hands turned icy cold.

"No, I didn't text you!" Shayla cried. "*Was* Mom in an accident?" she asked, obviously at a loss as to what to think.

Grabbing the wheel with both hands, Chris made a screeching U-turn in the middle of the block. His mind raced as he struggled to put together a plausible scenario of what was happening.

Only one thing occurred to him.

"Suzie."

Shayla was doing her best to follow him. "That CSI agent you brought with you to Uncle Andrew's?"

He didn't bother to answer. There was something far more urgent on his mind. "I'm going to need to have backup sent to Simpson's Airport right away."

"That's a private airport, isn't it?" Shayla questioned.

Again, he didn't reply. There was no time for a conversation or explanations. Right now he was too busy weaving in and out of traffic as cut-off, angered drivers leaned on their horns, blaring them at him.

"Listen very carefully, Shay. I need to have Warren Eldridge's private jet grounded," he told his sister. "He can't be allowed to take off. Understand?"

"The billionaire?" she asked. "You want me to keep his plane grounded? Hey, I'm good, but I'm not a miracle worker."

"Learn!" he ordered. "Do whatever you have to. Call the tower. But it can't take off until I get there!"

With that, he terminated the call and pressed down even harder on the accelerator.

Suzie came to.

She thought she could hear a voice somewhere in the distance. An indistinct voice.

She tried to focus, but she couldn't make out what the voice was saying. Everything was still spinning around in her head and she ached all over. Especially her head. She didn't remember getting hit. Just this strange, hot, stinging sensation at the side of her neck.

Coming to, Suzie gradually became aware of her surroundings.

There weren't any.

She was in some sort of an enclosed, confined space. A very *small* space.

Her adrenaline was rising at an alarming rate. She didn't like small, tight spaces. *Really* didn't like them.

Perspiration formed along the crown of her head

and she could hear her breathing growing shallow. She couldn't make herself stop.

It's just a space. The walls aren't closing in around you, she silently argued. *You're going to be okay.*

This was just temporary. She was going to get out of it, Suzie assured herself, doing her best not to panic. She was claustrophobic and there was a time when she couldn't even get on an elevator. She'd worked hard to get past that and she had, but now she felt waves of the fear coming back, wrapping around her.

She could feel her breathing growing labored.

Where *was* she?

She tried to yell and found that she couldn't. There was some sort of adhesive tape over her mouth—duct tape?—and even though her hands weren't bound, she still couldn't move them. She'd been stuffed into some kind of a box and her arms were bent behind her so that she wasn't able to do anything with her hands. Wasn't able to use them to make any sort of a sound.

The noise she'd thought she'd heard outside this box-like prison was fading away. Were they leaving her here?

Suddenly, she felt herself being shifted, moved. What was happening?

The next second, she realized that whatever she was in was being transported. Because of the angle, she almost felt as if her enclosure had been leaned against something.

Something with wheels. The swifter movement confirmed her feelings. She was being taken somewhere.

What was going on? Where was she and who was moving her?

Her mind, still dull from whatever had been injected into her, struggled to make sense out of what was happening.

They were moving faster. And the journey was really bumpy and unsettled. And then everything stopped. She'd stopped moving. Had they reached their destination?

And exactly where was that?

She emitted an almost animal-like sound through her nose as the dark enclosure she was in hit something hard. Had it been picked up and thrown? That was what it felt like.

Suzie still couldn't make sense out of what was going on, but she realized that if she tried hard enough, she could make a sound—a high-pitched, almost unearthly sound. That had to get someone's attention—if there was someone out there to hear her.

There just had to be!

She had to believe that there was someone out there so she continued her own version of screaming, even though her lips were sealed.

The only problem was she was getting dizzy because of the lack of air inside this prison she was in.

She hoped someone would hear her before she passed out.

Or asphyxiated.

* * *

Chris drove like a man possessed, only vaguely aware that he had broken every traffic rule ever written and most likely some that hadn't been passed yet. Twice he narrowly avoided crashing into another vehicle.

None of that registered. The only thing that mattered was that he get to the airport before Eldridge's jet took off.

Suzie had been right. Damn it, why hadn't he believed her?

He had no idea how the man had pulled it off, but he was certain that Eldridge had had one of his assistants send that text about his mother. Most likely in hopes that it would take not just Chris, but Suzie out of his office so that he could get away without any interference. But the billionaire obviously hadn't counted on Suzie's stubborn determination to bring him down for what he'd done.

To be honest, until just now, Chris had thought that she'd focused on Eldridge because she'd become so ultrasensitive about missing what was right out there in front of her. She'd done it once and he knew that she was obsessed about not doing it again. When she examined and reexamined everything the way she had, he'd just thought she was seeing things that weren't there.

But he'd been the blind one.

He'd been the blind one and Warren Eldridge the ultra-clever, ultra-devious one. Philanthropy was just a cover. The man was sicker than anyone ever suspected.

Why hadn't he seen it?

Why hadn't he realized that he'd left Suzie in the lion's den like some kind of a sacrificial lamb? And why hadn't he seen that she actually matched the billionaire's favored victim of choice?

Suzie was blonde, willowy and young. Exactly the type Eldridge was attracted to.

Exactly the type he killed.

Chris could feel his heart racing, and he sent up a prayer. He had to get to the airport in time. He just *had* to.

Within minutes, he was driving onto the property. A chain-link fence ran along the length of it, meant to keep trespassers from accessing the private airfield.

Chris never hesitated; he drove right through the fence, bringing it down and dragging a section of it before it fell off to the side.

It never even slowed him down.

Squinting, he saw Eldridge's jet. It was still stationary.

He drove straight for it.

If he was wrong, if he'd miscalculated and the serial killer wasn't Eldridge, if the billionaire didn't have Suzie, it meant the end of his career and most likely his freedom. Not even his family could help him if he was wrong.

But something in his gut kept telling him that he wasn't.

He saw the billionaire's stretch limo on the field right beside the jet.

Driving closer, he saw that Eldridge had disembarked and that two of the assistants he had seen dancing to the man's attendance were struggling to take out the old, banged-up steamer trunk that had been in the man's office.

Suzie was nowhere to be seen.

Had Eldridge already killed her, and had her body disposed of somewhere?

Rage began to swell up in Chris's chest. So much so that he was having trouble breathing. He'd never wanted to kill a man before.

He did now.

He brought his vehicle to a skidding, screeching stop right in front of the limo.

Eldridge turned in his direction, his expression more bored than anything. The man was one cool bastard, Chris thought.

"More questions, Detective?" Eldridge asked him in a disinterested voice.

He didn't have time for this charade. "Where is she?" Chris demanded.

"That young—what did you call her?—investigator?" Eldridge asked, as if he was trying to summon an image to his mind and having trouble doing so. "Why, she left right after you did."

"I don't believe you," Chris growled. "Where is she?"

They were standing close together now. Chris was almost the same height as Eldridge, and although at least twenty years older, Eldridge was in good shape and looked as if he could take care of himself if it came to that. Chris could almost taste the blows that could be exchanged.

Eldridge shrugged, his custom-made jacket moving like a second skin. "I haven't the vaguest idea."

The animal-like noise that came out of the trunk just then immediately drew Chris's attention. Something inside the large container began to bang against the lid.

Was she in there?

"Open the trunk," Chris ordered the billionaire. He was aware that the man's two assistants were watching him warily.

"It's my mother's old steamer trunk," Eldridge told him, making no move to comply. "It's filled with old bric-a-brac and I take it everywhere I go. If I open it, everything's going to come spilling out, and I don't have the time to waste having it gathered up." He drew himself up imperially, his eyes narrowing as he glared at Chris. "Now unless you want to suddenly find yourself conducting traffic in the middle of downtown Oakland, because I assure you I can make it happen, you will let me get my luggage on board my jet and—"

Chris didn't waste his breath arguing. He pulled out his weapon and pointed it at the billionaire. Confronted with this new twist, Elridge's assistants stepped back, silently indicating that they weren't part of anything illegal as they nervously looked at the detective.

"I said *open it*!" To punctuate his command, he cocked his weapon. *"Now!"*

Eldridge stood his ground. "You're being ridiculous, Detective."

Chris fired a shot to the right of the man's shoulder. Eldridge yelped indignantly.

"I'm not going to ask you again," Chris warned.

"You are going to regret this!" Eldridge swore.

"Not half as much as you are unless you open that lid," he told Eldridge, cocking his weapon a second time.

"All right, all right! I'm opening it." After unlocking the trunk, Eldridge threw off the latch.

The next second, the trunk flew open.

Not waiting for the lid to be pulled off, Suzie had pushed it up with the top of her head. Staggering to her feet now, she drew her right arm back, made a fist and swung at Eldridge's chin with every fiber of her somewhat limited strength.

Stunned and completely unprepared for the blow, Eldridge fell, unconscious, to the ground.

Her hands now free, Suzie yanked the tape off her mouth and threw it angrily on the ground.

"What kept you?" she demanded, glaring at Chris.

"Got caught in traffic," he answered, not trusting his voice for a moment to say anything serious. "You know how it is."

Weapon still ready and pointed at the unconscious billionaire, Chris put the other arm around Suzie to help her out of the trunk. She felt as if she was shaking.

"Are you all right?" he asked.

Suzie couldn't take her eyes off the unconscious figure on the ground. She wouldn't allow herself to think about what had almost happened, or what *could* have happened. Only about what had just happened. Chris had come for her.

He'd rescued her.

"Never better," she told him.

He sincerely had his doubts about that. "Your heart is hammering like a hummingbird's," he pointed out.

"That's just because I'm standing next to you," she cracked.

The sound of approaching sirens swelled, growing louder, telling her that they weren't going to be alone for long.

So she kissed him.

And then she almost sank to her knees—and would have, if he hadn't had his arm around her.

Chapter 20

The next moment, squad cars were pulling up, forming what could pass for a circle around the black stretch limousine and Warren Eldridge, as well as his two quaking assistants. Suzie instantly straightened and, grasping Chris's arm, managed to get back up to her feet.

If looks could kill, Chris thought, the groggy billionaire would have easily mowed down the police personnel emerging from the cruisers.

"You wouldn't dare," Eldridge warned, getting to his feet. His eyes blazed as he issued the edict to the two law enforcement agents who were closest to him.

"Yeah, we would," Chris answered. Turning to Suzie, he held out a set of handcuffs. "You want to do the honors?"

There was no missing the pleasure that came into her eyes. "I'd be thrilled," she told him.

Taking them, she circled Eldridge until she was directly behind him. Then, as other officers on the scene trained their weapons at the man, she pulled his hands back and cuffed his wrists.

And then she said what she'd wanted to say since she had first zeroed in on the billionaire as a suspect. "Warren Eldridge, you're under arrest for murder."

Eldridge surprised them by laughing. "You'll never prove it!"

"I wouldn't go betting your considerable empire on that if I were you," Suzie said with sheer contempt. She called over the closest uniformed policeman. "Read him his rights and take Mr. Eldridge down to central booking. The charge is murder—multiple murders," she amended. "I'll supply the list of names later."

The policeman took charge of the prisoner, leading him to a squad car as he said, "You have the right to remain silent. If you give up this right, everything you say can…"

"You'll be sorry," Eldridge called over his shoulder, taunting her.

"Not a chance," Suzie retorted.

She waited until Eldridge was removed from the scene before she turned toward Chris. As satisfying as it was to see the man in handcuffs, she was well aware that this was just the first step.

"We're still going to have to get a confession out of him," she said.

This was far from being wrapped up with a bow, but at this point, Chris was feeling pretty good about the eventual outcome.

"I think kidnapping a federal agent and stuffing her into a trunk is a pretty good starting point. Speaking of the steamer trunk, we're sure to find some interesting DNA there. Guys like Eldridge always trip themselves up one way or another."

Suzie looked at the departing squad car with Eldridge in it. "I certainly hope so."

Shayla O'Bannon had arrived as part of the backup crew. Since she had been instrumental in calling them together, she temporarily took the lead. Which meant she had to take abbreviated statements from Suzie and Chris on what had gone down prior to the officers' arrival.

She made quick notes on her tablet, then closed the lid. "I'll get the rest when you two make your official reports," she told them. About to leave, she turned toward her brother. "By the way, I called Ma just to make sure she was okay. She was. How did that creep know to have someone text you about her rig crashing—and pretending to be me, of all things?"

"He used your name to make it more believable," Chris guessed. "No telling what kind of access to information someone of Eldridge's stature and reputation has."

Suzie spoke up. "Eldridge bragged that he did his homework on both of us."

"Sounds like his interrogation is going to go on

for a long time," Shayla speculated. "Well, I'd better go read those two butt-kissers their rights before I take them in as accessories," she added just before she walked away.

Suzie turned to Chris the second his sister was gone. "I want to be the one to question Eldridge."

He understood how she felt, but there was no way anyone was going to let that happen.

"You know you can't, Suzie," he pointed out. "You could have been his next victim."

Suzie waved away the possibility of what he was suggesting. "All right, so I can't interrogate him," she said, relenting. "But I want to be in the room when you question him."

Chris didn't want to discuss that now. He'd come very close to losing her—losing her after just having realized what she meant to him—and right now, all he cared about was making sure that she was all right. That that psychopath hadn't hurt her. Because in his opinion, Suzie was looking way too pale.

Maybe that SOB had done something to her while he was stuffing her into the trunk, Chris thought, worried.

"You'll be in a room, all right," he told her. "A hospital room, getting checked out."

Suzie pressed her lips together, struggling to cope with her impatience. She'd gone through a lot just now and she wasn't about to add poking and prodding to the list. She appreciated that Chris was concerned, but she knew what she needed, and it wasn't being some doctor's lab project.

"I'm fine, O'Bannon," she insisted.

"Well, you look like death warmed over," he informed her.

That was *not* what she needed to hear. "Nice to see you, too," she retorted.

Putting his hands on her shoulders to anchor her in place, Chris tried to reason with her. "Suzie, he almost killed you."

"But he didn't," she stated.

She was missing the point, Chris thought. "If I hadn't arrived just then—"

She cut him off again. "But you did, and reality is all that counts here, not 'maybes' and 'could haves,'" she insisted.

He was trying hard not to lose his temper. Almost losing her had frayed it practically to the breaking point.

"Look, playing the superheroine is cute up to a point, Suzie Q, but you're going to the hospital even if I have to throw you over my shoulder and carry you all the way there."

She put her hands up, ready to make him back off. "I'm not as weak as I look, O'Bannon."

"Maybe so, but I'm willing to bet that my son's still stronger than a slip of a girl who probably weighs all of a hundred and ten pounds if she's carrying rocks in her pockets."

Suzie whirled around to find Maeve O'Bannon standing right behind her. Had his entire family decided to show up?

Chris was the first to put it into words. "Ma, what are you doing here?"

"When Shayla called, saying strange things about my having been in an accident, I got her to fill me in on what was going on. Naturally, I decided to see who was using my name in vain," she told her son. "I drove over in the rig just in case you shot the underhanded jackass. Since I don't see any blood anywhere, why don't we use my vehicle to take your friend here to the ER?" And then she added, "I overheard," in case there was some doubt about the reason behind her offer.

Now she was going to have to ward off two of them, Suzie thought with an inward sigh. "There's no need, Mrs. O'Bannon," she told her as cheerfully as she could. "I'm fine."

"It's Maeve, dear, please," his mother said. "And put an old woman's mind to rest," she requested, putting a hand on Suzie's shoulder. "It never hurts to get checked out after going through an ordeal." Her tone was warm, friendly, but there was no mistaking the underlying steel in her words.

Suzie found herself being directed toward the ambulance. "I'm fine," she protested again, making one last-ditch effort, even though in her gut she knew it was futile.

"I know, I know," Maeve said, placating her, "but I'll feel much better when someone wearing a stethoscope around their neck tells me that." She ushered Suzie into her rig. "My brother Sean has glowing words to say about you, claims that you have all this potential. Shame if that potential didn't get to be realized."

Maeve glanced over her shoulder to see that her son was right behind them. She smiled and nodded. "Never could say no to an ambulance ride, could you?"

Chris helped Suzie into the back of the ambulance, then climbed in himself. "I'm just coming along to make sure she doesn't escape before you get to the hospital."

"I don't make any stops," Maeve reminded him. "Not even for the lights."

He looked at Suzie. "That wouldn't stop her."

Just what did he take her for? "Quit looking at me that way. I'm not about to leap out of a moving vehicle," Suzie protested.

"I know that," he replied cheerfully. "And I'm coming along to make sure you don't."

She watched as the doors were closed behind her. All she needed was a little rest. Why wouldn't they believe her? "This isn't necessary."

"You're outnumbered, Suzie Q. Humor us," she heard his mother say from the front of the rig, just before she started it up.

"Is everyone in your family this pushy?" Suzie asked in a low voice, once they were on the road.

"Not everyone," he answered. "But you don't hear much from them," he added with a grin.

"It figures," she murmured under her breath, resigning herself to the ordeal ahead.

* * *

"Satisfied?" Suzie demanded.

She was still in the ER, but finally back in her own clothes. The doctor on call had given her an exam and put her through a battery of tests, before telling her that aside from a few minor cuts and bruises, she had suffered no real adverse effects from her ordeal and was free to go home.

She had addressed her rhetorical question to Chris. "The doctor says I'm fine and I can leave now."

Chris glanced over his shoulder to make sure the curtains were securely pulled around her small enclosure. Seeing that they were, he moved closer to her. Rather than saying anything in response, he just took Suzie in his arms and kissed her.

Long and hard.

Kissed her until she could feel her knees threatening to give out again the way they had earlier, but for an entirely different reason.

Just in case, she braced herself against him as he drew his head back.

"Now are you satisfied?" she asked breathlessly.

He continued holding her. There was a smile in his eyes that radiated down to his lips. "Oh, I'm just getting started, Suzie Q."

She didn't know what to think, or what Chris was capable of, under the circumstances. They'd both been through the wringer in the last few hours.

"Not here," she half protested, half pleaded.

"No, not here," he agreed. Very gently, Chris

framed her face with his palms. "This is going to take a lot longer than just an afternoon—or an evening," he added, when he saw the question in her eyes.

"What are you saying?"

Since he had already signed all the necessary papers to check her out, Chris threaded his fingers through hers and led her from the cubicle. "What I'm saying is that I think I'm going to need a lifetime."

She felt like she was just stumbling along behind him, down the hall. "What?"

He'd pulled up his vehicle to the hospital doors. Shayla had driven it to the ER for him. He brought her over to it now and held the passenger door open for her as she got in.

"You know how some things take a long time to develop, while other things just come right at you, riding a thunderbolt?" he asked, getting in on his side. He paused to look at her. "You're my thunderbolt, Suzie Q."

After reaching for her seat belt, she winced as she pulled it into place. "I was the one getting oxygen-deprived in that ratty trunk, not you. But you're the one not making any sense."

"Yeah, I am." Starting up his car, he pulled away from the hospital. "Think about it," he told her. Then he repeated the phrase with emphasis, as if giving her something more to consider. "*Think* about it. I don't need an answer today, or tomorrow, or anytime soon. I need an answer whenever you feel like giving it."

"An answer," she repeated uncertainly.

"An answer."

She thought she knew what he was saying, but this was one time she didn't want to jump to a conclusion—especially if it was the wrong one. "Might help if I had a question to go with it."

He spared her a quick glance. "You already know the question."

She wanted it spelled out. "Pretend I don't."

"Okay, Suzie Q, I've just been to hell and back, thinking that maniac killed you. It made me realize that nothing else matters if you're not here to go through it with me." He didn't even pause to take a breath. "Suzie Q, will you marry me?"

"Okay."

Just like that? He stared at her, then realized he was driving and needed to watch the road. "Okay, you'll marry me?"

"No, okay, now I have something to think about."

She was yanking on his chain. "I left myself open for that."

"Yup."

He could hear the grin in her voice. She was alive and he could forgive her any one of a number of things because of that. "That's all right, I can wait. You take all the time you need."

"And you don't care?" she asked him suddenly.

He was having trouble keeping up with her. "That you take all the time you need?" he questioned.

"No, you don't care about who my father is?" She needed to get this cleared up once and for all.

"As long as he doesn't come on the honeymoon

with us, no, I don't care who your father is," Chris said in no uncertain terms. "You're not your father, Suzie. You're you and that's all I care about."

She realized that she believed him. "And you're willing to wait for any answer?"

"As long as it takes," he assured her—and then added with a grin, "As long as we can fool around now and again while I'm waiting."

She knew for a fact that it was too late to go in to the precinct. Which made her think about going home—and what that meant. "How about now?"

Chris grinned again. "Works for me."

"Me, too." So saying, she reached up and turned on the siren.

They ran the siren only in an emergency. "What are you doing?"

"Drive faster," she told him. "Otherwise, I can't be held accountable for my actions, and I might just jump you right here in the car—which in turn might cause a collision and a possible multi-car pileup. And that'll be all your fault."

She really was going to be all right, he thought, relieved. "You do have a way of painting a picture," he told her with a laugh.

"You want a picture painted? How about this one?" she asked, just before she leaned in to whisper into his ear. She told him, in detail, exactly what she intended to do the minute they reached her apartment.

Chris pressed down on the accelerator as far as it would go. "Driving faster," he announced.

The sound of her laughter warmed his heart.

Epilogue

Suzie caught herself clutching the armrests of the chair she was sitting in. A chair that was facing the chief of detectives' desk, while he sat on the other side.

Part of the problem was that she had no idea what she was doing here or why she had been summoned. It helped a little that Chris was already here, sitting in the other chair, but it still didn't clear up the matter of *why* for her.

She'd already met Brian Cavanaugh informally, at the family gathering she'd attended, and of course she knew the man by sight. Most of the people who worked at the precinct did. But that still didn't explain why he'd asked to see her.

Had Warren Eldridge made good on his threat and had his legion of lawyers sue the police department?

It had been only three days since the psychopath had locked her in that steamer trunk, but things had moved fast. The DNA results had come back a match and she had had to tell Mrs. Wilson that the unidentified "Jane Doe" had turned out to be her daughter. Then had held the woman as she cried. If Suzie hadn't hated Eldridge before, she did now.

Had the bastard called in favors to get the chief of d's and everyone else connected to this case fired?

She hadn't a clue.

"You know, you don't have to hold on to the armrests so hard. The chair's not going anywhere," Brian told her gently.

She loosened her grip, but it took effort. "Yes, sir. I mean no, sir."

Brian laughed kindly, clearly doing his best to put her at ease. "Relax, Agent Quinn, you're not facing a firing squad. And by the way, breathing is not optional." He turned toward his nephew. "Tell her to breathe, Detective O'Bannon. Your mother will have my head if I have to call the paramedics."

Chris smiled. "Better do as the man says, Suzie Q. He's usually right about things."

Her eyes never leaving the chief, Suzie took a deep breath, then slowly released it. Her pulse was still tap-dancing in her wrists, but the tempo was beginning to slow a bit.

"That's better," Brian said with approval. "Now,

do you know why you and Detective O'Bannon are here?"

She took a stab at it. She'd found that meeting things head-on was the best way. "You're firing me?"

By his expression, she realized that she'd taken the chief by surprise.

"Good Lord, no," he said. "Why would I want to fire you?"

Then he wasn't firing her, she thought, still confused even as she answered his question. "Because I'm responsible for Warren Eldridge suing everyone in the department."

"*Threatening* to sue everyone," Brian corrected. "Big difference. No, you're here because I wanted you and Detective O'Bannon to be the first to know that because of you, the grand jury has just indicted Warren Eldridge on over thirty counts of murder."

"How many?" she cried, stunned. She'd come up with eleven victims on last count.

"Thirty, but the number is still growing," Brian told her. "Turns out that our local philanthropist has been at this a long time, not just here but on the East Coast, as well as everywhere in between. Apparently every place that Warren Eldridge held a fund-raiser or gave a sizable donation to some foundation, he left that area with one less person in their midst. Thanks to one of his assistants turning state's evidence in exchange for a reduced sentence, we're finding bodies everywhere."

She didn't even want to picture that. It was her father all over again—with one notable exception.

"But he has all those lawyers on retainer," Suzie reminded the chief. "They'll be able to explain away anything."

"I'm not so sure. The judge issued us a search warrant for all of Eldridge's homes. Seems that in his panic room in the house up in Lake Tahoe Eldridge had a wall safe where he kept the souvenirs he collected from each kill."

"Souvenirs?" Chris echoed. "What did he take?"

Brian smiled at Suzie. "Actually, Agent Quinn directed our attention to it."

She had no idea what the chief was referring to. "I did?"

The man nodded. "Unlike the other victims, Eldridge hadn't taken your clothing yet, but he had already taken something. You accused him of stealing the cross your mother gave you. Turns out that each of his victims wore a cross—a cross that he subsequently kept after he killed them."

Brian paused to reflect for a moment. "Maybe that was what set him off to begin with. They all resembled the mother who never had any time for him, and they wore a small gold cross, just as she did. To him that cross represented the last word in hypocrisy. It was his 'trigger' so to speak. That safe of his in the panic room was filled with the crosses he collected from his victims."

Brian rose and came around to the other side of his desk, taking Suzie's hands in his. "I'm sorry you had to get banged up in the process, but nice work, Agent Quinn. *Very* nice work."

"Thank you, sir."

Releasing her hands, he leaned against the desk at his back. "Now I want you and Detective O'Bannon to take the rest of the week off. I think after what you've both been through, you two *more* than deserve a little downtime."

She didn't want to be singled out, although she appreciated why he was doing it. "Just doing our jobs, sir," Suzie told him.

"And I'm just doing mine," he countered. "Go home, both of you," he told them. "I don't want to see either one of you until Saturday."

"Saturday?" Chris questioned.

"Yes, at the former chief of police's house. We've just brought down one hell of a notorious serial killer. If that's not something to celebrate, then I don't know what is. Well, actually, knowing my brother, I do, but this is still definitely worth celebrating and he'll want you to be there," he said, looking directly at Suzie.

She knew there was no way out of it, and surprisingly, she didn't want there to be. "Yes, sir."

"Now go," Brian ordered.

They were quick to comply.

"So, you haven't been to my place yet," Chris said as they got out of the elevator on the first floor. "How about you come over and I'll make you dinner?"

Exiting the building, she looked at him in surprise. "You cook?"

He'd promised himself that he would always be

truthful with her. “Not exactly, but I microwave with the best of them.”

Suzy nodded. “Okay, you talked me into it.”

Dinner wasn’t spectacular, but it was quick, which was just as well, since she was no more interested in eating than it turned out that Chris was.

Dessert held a far greater allure.

“You know, woman, if we keep doing this on a regular basis—and I sincerely hope we do—I’m afraid you’re going to wear me out before the year’s over,” Chris told her as he struggled to catch the breath she had taken away from him. Lovemaking with Suzie was a constant surprise. She not only kept up, half the time she took the lead.

He was struck again by the fact that he had never met anyone quite like her.

Rather than curl up next to him, the way he’d thought she would, Suzie drew herself up until her torso was against his and she was looking down into his face.

He had no idea what to expect. When he looked at her with an unspoken question in his eyes, she said, “Yes.”

“Yes?” Chris repeated uncertainly.

She nodded and said yes again.

Still no clue, he thought. He refused to take anything for granted. “Okay, yes what?”

“You asked me a question in the hospital,” she reminded him.

He stared at her, momentarily drawing a blank.

And then, just like that, it came back to him. Chris scrambled into a sitting position, almost throwing her off balance. Did she possibly mean…?

"Are you talking about when I asked you to marry me?"

She reminded him of the circumstances. "You said I could take all the time I wanted to answer you."

"Not in those exact words, but yes, that was the gist of it. Is that your answer?" he asked, trying not to sound as if he was pushing her, but at the same time anxious for the wait to be over. He'd never thought of himself as the possessive type, but he did want her exclusively to himself.

Had she waited too long? She wasn't sure if she was on stable ground. "Unless you'd rather that it wasn't," she said, giving him a way out.

Chris sighed. "I'm going to have to take you back to the hospital and make sure they didn't miss any signs of a concussion," he told her. "Right after I finish showing you what's in store for you on our wedding night."

Suzie slid back against the bed. "I can hardly wait," she breathed.

He gathered her into his arms. "Lucky for you, my mother taught me never to keep a lady waiting."

She grinned. "I think I love your mother."

"And I love you," he told her, his voice growing very serious.

"I love you more," she said, just as he was about to kiss her.

"Oh, good," he declared, the serious moment gone. "I love a competition."

And then he proceeded to show her just how much.

* * * * *

Don't forget previous titles in the CAVANAUGH JUSTICE *series:*

CAVANAUGH COLD CASE
CAVANAUGH OR DEATH
HOW TO SEDUCE A CAVANAUGH
CAVANAUGH FORTUNE
CAVANAUGH STRONG

Available now from Mills & Boon Romantic Suspense!